Praise for

EPIC ELLISONS

COSMOS CAMP and LAMAR GILES

"*Epic Ellisons: Cosmos Camp* will take you on a rocket ride of sci-fi wonder, mystery, and fun!"

—**Jeff Kinney**, #1 *New York Times* bestselling author of the **Diary of a Wimpy Kid** series

"If Lamar Giles wrote *Epic Ellisons: Cosmos Camp*, then I want to read it. Yes, he's that good!"

—**Chris Grabenstein**, #1 *New York Times* bestselling author of the **Mr. Lemoncello's Library** series

"Do you like space-travel, time-travel, robots, rockets, gizmos, and whozeewhatzits of every variety? Do you like hi-octane mysteries getting solved by super-smart detectives? Do you like to laugh, and think, and care a whole lot about the characters when you're reading? A lot of books claim to have it all, but it's been a long time since a book has come anywhere as close as *Epic Ellisons: Cosmos Camp*. Oh, I just thought of something the book is missing: even a single second of boredom!"

—**Carlos Hernandez**, Pura Belpré Award–winning author of *Sal and Gabi Break the Universe*

"Every child, regardless of background, deserves adventure void of trauma. Every child deserves to exist in magical spaces where their imaginations and familial bonds will them into heroism. . . . And I, for one, am grateful to Giles . . . for that reminder."

—**Jason Reynolds**, #1 *New York Times* bestselling
and Newbery Honor-winning author of **Stuntboy, in the Meantime** for **The Last Last-Day-of-Summer**

"With total mastery, Giles creates . . . an exuberant vortex of weirdness, where the commonplace sits cheek by jowl with the utterly fantastic, and populates it with memorable characters."

—**Kirkus Reviews** (starred review) for
The Last Last-Day-of-Summer

"Giles interjects affecting realism with themes of reconciliation, family, identity, and destiny."

—**Publishers Weekly** (starred review) for
The Last Last-Day-of-Summer

"Anchored by its genuine characters and buoyed by its true fun . . . An adventure with staying power."

—**ALA Booklist** (starred review) for
The Last Last-Day-of-Summer

"Thrilling and heartfelt . . . An absolute first purchase."

—**School Library Journal** (starred review) for
The Last Mirror on the Left

EPIC ELLISONS

COSMOS CAMP

LAMAR GILES

Illustrations by Morgan Bissant

VERSIFY
An Imprint of HarperCollinsPublishers

Versify® is an imprint of HarperCollins Publishers.

Epic Ellisons: Cosmos Camp
Text copyright © 2023 by Lamar Giles
Illustrations copyright © 2023 by Morgan Bissant
ISBN 978-0-35-842337-9

Typography by Corina Lupp

23 24 25 26 27 LBC 5 4 3 2 1

First Edition

EPIC ELLISONS

COSMOS CAMP

For the stargazers and trailblazers

Don't let anyone rob you of your imagination, your creativity, or your curiosity. It's your place in the world; it's your life. Go on and do all you can with it, and make it the life you want to live.

—DR. MAE JEMISON,
first African American woman
astronaut in space

COUNTDOWN
36:23:19:02

1

Some Time Apart

Victoria and Evangeleen Ellison—"Wiki" and "Leen" to their friends, or "Epic Ellisons" to folks who needed saving around Logan County—had never, ever been apart. Not for any amount of time worth mentioning anyway, unless it was their daddy doing the talking.

They were twins born seven minutes apart. Daddy loved telling their In The Hospital story. "That seven minutes might be the longest you two were separated for, shoot, the first three or four years of your life. It's funny because Wiki didn't even cry until Leen was born laughing. One of the nurses cried too because, believe it or not, a baby born laughing is a little creepy. No offense, sweet pea."

"It's almost impossible to offend me, Daddy," Leen said every time.

Daddy always told it like he was revealing a secret, though everyone in the family knew the tale by heart. Even Uncle Percy who mostly *pretended* to listen to people while texting or scrolling through pictures on ThunkleGram.

"You two"—Daddy would slap his thigh as he finished—"have been roommates since you were in your mama's belly. Ain't that fun?"

Then he'd laugh like he'd told a joke. It wasn't fun or funny though, only true.

While he laughed, Mama would flick her eyes between her unamused, barely smiling daughters. Leen may not have noticed because it's not the sort of thing she cared much about, but Wiki couldn't help catching those quick glances. Thanks to her photographic memory and ability to process information computer fast, Wiki had become an expert at reading faces—the tics and tells. The message on their mother's face was *BIG and **bold***. It said: *Sorry, girls, boys just don't get it. Not even when they're old like your dad.*

School was over. Had been for about a week. Those days leading up to D. Franklin Middle School's final bell had not been the ones that had Leen most excited. If anything, the last day of school meant she'd have seven more whole boring, unoccupied days until the one she'd really been waiting for.

When she left for Cosmos Camp.

Okay, that week between the end of school and her last night in Logan County wasn't *totally* boring. She and Wiki helped the Legendary Alston Boys defeat some mutant moles. They also got to stay out until 8:30 one night and have gelato with the boys, which definitely wasn't a double date because Mama said they were way too young to date and Uncle Percy sat in the corner of the Riches Brew coffee shop the entire time, pointing at Otto and Sheed with his spoon while mouthing silent threats.

So the week was mildly amusing—the gelato more than the mutant moles—but with less than twelve hours between her and her summer away, Leen found herself jittery with excitement. Sleep would not come easy. Thankfully, Wiki was happy to sit with her, help keep her calm, until they went their separate ways.

"You're going to learn so much about all of that," Wiki said, pointing broadly at the sky dotted with mysterious pin-pricks of light.

I know, Leen thought, giddy with the prospect of it all.

They were in their favorite spot, atop an out-of-commission tractor that belonged to their grandparents, in the middle of a cornfield. Though the tires were dry rotted and stalks sprouted from the engine block, the hood, when covered with their favorite blanket, made a great spot for stargazing.

Slathered in minty bug repellent, with flashlights resting between them, the girls craned their necks, always awed by such perfectly summer Logan County nights and their marvelous view from their tiny, tiny section of the universe.

"I wish you could come," Leen said. It wasn't true but felt like the right thing to say.

"Cosmos Camp sounds fun, but that's your thing. I'll be plenty busy here until you get back."

That was also a lie. At least partially. There'd be a ton of work around the farm, like always, so "busy" was true. Cosmos Camp sounded a little fun, but Wiki knew she was overselling that part. She wasn't *trying* to deceive her sister with exaggerated enthusiasm as much as keep something important to herself. A secret that she hadn't uttered aloud because she'd been afraid to.

Wiki was looking forward to a summer alone.

She'd miss Leen, sure. No question. But . . . Leen could be exhausting.

Her unpredictable inventions that she couldn't always control. The way she seemed unaware of how dangerous some of her experiments were. Or who had to help clean up every single mess she made (that would be Wiki, ten times out of ten). Mostly, it was fine. Part of the twin contract. In a county as strange as Logan, sometimes you needed a little unpredictability to save your butt.

4

However . . .

Wiki sure was looking forward to seeing what a summer on her own was like. Maybe she'd hate it. Maybe she'd desperately miss Leen and count the days until her dear sister returned.

There was only one way to find out.

"Oh! I made you something!" Leen said, rooting through the bag wedged between them. The bag Wiki had wondered about, but was afraid to ask.

Alarmed, Wiki scooted sideways, almost falling off the tractor, and asked, "Where does it rate on the LMDS?"

The LMDS was the Leen's Machines Danger Scale, a ten-point range for gauging the safety (or lack thereof) of Leen's inventions. It went from one (Not Dangerous at All, Probably) to ten (The Army's on the Phone!).

"Solid three. Or five," Leen said, freeing the device from the sack.

"Ummm . . ."

"Just wait."

She produced a stainless-steel rectangle embedded with some sort of screen. It seemed too chunky for a typical tablet—also, Leen rarely built anything typical. When she tapped the Power button, bringing the screen to life, displaying one of Wiki's favorite photos, all became clear.

Wiki said, "A digital picture frame?"

"Yep!"

That was . . . unremarkable. Not in a bad way. It was a thoughtful gift, particularly since it displayed one of Wiki's favorite photos—the two of them in a game of tag, Leen chasing Wiki. Wiki had the ability to recall that picture in her head at any given time, but she preferred seeing it for real, outside of her memory.

She felt the slightest urge to cry over the sweet, sweet present. "You're the one going away. Shouldn't I give *you* something?"

Leen waved off the question. "There's more."

Uh-oh. Sudden fear dried up Wiki's tears.

Leen pressed another button, and the photo literally leapt off the screen. A holographic projection sprang forth, so a second Wiki and Leen, frozen in midstride, now stood before the tractor. Somehow the photo had become life-sized models of the twins, seemingly as solid as real people!

Wiki hopped off the tractor, inspecting the perfect projections closely. Wiki had seen her sister produce amazing things from next to nothing, but this was one of her more impressive innovations.

Leen, who'd taken to wearing a discreet gauntlet beneath her left sleeve that acted as a sort of all-in-one control for any of her nearby inventions, tapped a command into her wearable tech, and a projection shot from her general wrist area.

6

Another, slightly fuzzier version of the same holograph. "My gauntlet doesn't have quite the capability of the frame, so the definition isn't as high, but you see, we both have this same photo anytime we want it."

"This is great!" said Wiki. "Why'd you give it a five on the LMDS?"

As if on cue, a spark flew from the frame like a tiny meteorite. The hologram flickered from existence, and that spark landed on a dry cornstalk, setting it ablaze.

Quickly, Wiki stomped the fire out, saving all the other dry stalks around it. So it goes. She took the powered-down frame from Leen. "Thank you for this. It's very thoughtful. I maybe won't activate the holograms while you're away."

"You aren't going to get bored doing double chores every day?" Leen said, genuinely concerned their parents would work Wiki into an early grave since she'd be the only one here.

Wiki shook her head, but hesitantly. "When Uncle Percy told them he was hitting the road this summer to try and bring in more trucking money, they put out an ad for some farmhands. There will be help."

Leen's shoulders hunched a bit. Tense. "Will that be expensive?"

About as expensive as everything else was these days. Or so Wiki gathered from the late-night conversations—that were sometimes arguments—Mama and Daddy thought they were whispering. Still, she told another lie. "I don't think so."

"Good," Leen said, sounding relieved, though she didn't quite relax again. Instead, she changed the subject. "You think you'll hang with Otto and Sheed much?"

Wiki shrugged. "Don't know. I don't really have a plan." *And it's glorious!* she shouted inside her head.

Happy that Wiki would be mostly okay, and making herself believe Mama and Daddy weren't struggling to pay for everything a farm needed folks to pay for, there was one thing that still worried Leen. "You going to do okay with those bad dreams?"

Wiki's joyful anticipation decreased by half. "They're not really *bad*. Mostly strange."

"You toss and turn hard. Sometimes you yell."

"I do not."

She did. Leen knew because that's when she'd climb in bed with Wiki and hug her until she calmed down. No need to fight about it, though. At least Leen didn't want to. What would an argument change? After tomorrow morning, they'd have to work on their own problems in their own ways for a while.

The silence between them stretched. Wiki said, "You need to get some sleep. Big day. Let's head back, but first . . ."

Wiki snatched her ThunklePhone from her shirt pocket and held it high so she and Leen were shoulder to shoulder in selfie view.

"A new one to remember you by," Wiki said, tapping the screen with her thumb and triggering the flash.

That—the sentiment, not the flash—almost brought Leen to tears. She knew Wiki didn't need a camera to remember anything. So she must really love looking at Leen's smiling face.

The feeling was mutual.

It was a short walk through the field back to their house, where light glowed from every window. They clopped inside, kicking off their shoes at the door, and only barely registered Mama and Daddy talking in excited tones to someone on the phone.

Mama interrupted whatever conversation they were having and yelled, "Girls, is that you? Come in here, please."

The girls exchanged wary looks and entered the living room where their parents sat side by side on the couch with Mama's ThunklePhone resting on the coffee table, the screen glowing in speaker mode.

Daddy grinned his goofiest grin. "They just came in."

Wiki got more wary. *Whoever they are talking to, the conversation was about us?*

Leen simply chirped a cheerful, "Hello!"

From the phone, a woman said, "Hey there, girls. Y'all are just in time for some great news."

Wiki's memory did its thing, sorting through every voice she'd ever heard. In person. On TV. In a song. Overlaying those with the one from the phone, making instant comparisons. That voice belonged to Anna Thunkle, and Wiki's brain churned some more.

Anna was someone Wiki had never met in person but who had deep ties to the county they lived in. Anna grew up in the town of Fry, the town known as the beating heart of Logan County. Her father used to own Archie's Hardware on Main Street. These days people knew Anna as the richest woman in the world . . .

. . . because she was married to the richest man, a certain Logan County native and tech genius by the name of Petey Thunkle. Founder of PeteyTech.

Their company was responsible for most of the technology people used today. Everything from the ThunklePhones people carried to the Thunk-Tok social media app where people posted cool hair tutorials and funny dance videos to the Thulu streaming service where the Ellisons watched most of the shows and movies they enjoyed. The company did so many things. Including, the annual Cosmos Camp Leen was about to attend.

So this is about that, Wiki reasoned. Then thought, *Why'd she say* girls, *plural?*

Daddy waved them over to the couch, scooting so there was room for all four of them. Leen ran and jumped onto her usual seat cushion. Wiki's approach was slower, despite Mama bouncing in place and gushing with obvious glee.

Anna spoke while Wiki sat. "I was just telling your parents we're expanding the number of Cosmos Campers we're bringing in this season. With an extra slot, we thought it made sense to keep such an epic team together."

Leen's goofy smile vanished. "Excuse me?"

Wiki wasn't much happier. "Wait. You're not saying what I think you're saying, are you?"

"Is that you, Victoria? If so, then I'm definitely saying what you think I'm saying. Pack a bag! Tomorrow, you're coming to Cosmos Camp too!"

2
That Was...
Never a Thing

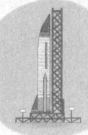

Mama clapped!

Dad pumped a fist in the air and hissed, "Yessss!"

Wiki and Leen were statues on the couch.

"Girls?" Anna said. "Pettygrew, did we lose 'em?"

"No, miss," said another voice on the line. Pettygrew. Whoever that was.

Wiki spoke up. "We're still here, Mrs. Thunkle."

"Call me Anna, please."

"Anna. This is a very cool offer, it's just—"

Leen interrupted her. "Wiki didn't even apply. How could she be the one who gets an extra slot if she didn't fill out the form or write an essay?" Leen's gaze whipped from Mama to Daddy. "Can you afford to send both of us?"

They were good questions. The right questions. Yet something sharp in her sister's voice stung Wiki.

If anyone else detected Leen's prickliness, they didn't let on. Anna said, "Several factors played into our selection. *Your* essay was one of them!"

The smile that formed on Leen's face was a scary thing, like an earthquake cracking the ground. "Say what?"

"Oh, we adored what you wrote about the many adventures you and your sister have been on. The teamwork. The love. Plus, I'm a bit biased being from Logan County too. So I'm more than happy to have two hometown heroes like the Epic Ellisons at camp this year."

Wiki thought that was all fine and good . . . well, not really, but okay. Leen wrote an incredible essay. She was good at stuff like that. The other concern, the thing that loomed over all things Ellison lately, was still the money.

In one of the overheard conversations—or eavesdropped on, depending on how sneaky Wiki wanted to admit she was being—Daddy told Mama they were "stretching" to send Leen to Cosmos Camp, but it would be good for her because she'd be around the kinds of science and scientists she needed. Wiki knew that to be true. Being in Logan County their entire lives and having to work with scraps had made Leen incredibly innovative and resilient. A limit was still a limit, though, and there were only so many Leen could work around until, maybe, she decided it wasn't worth the effort. Yet "stretching" was what they'd learned in language arts class to be a euphemism, a word people substituted for something

13

harsh they didn't want to say. In this case, it meant Mama and Daddy had a hard time affording the cost of Cosmos Camp. They'd have a harder time affording it when it was multiplied by two.

"The thing is," Wiki began, ready to decline the invite in a way that wouldn't embarrass Mama and Daddy, which simply meant being honest because she had no desire to attend Cosmos Camp, "I don't wanna—"

"Keep you waiting!" said Daddy. "We're going to get Wiki packed and ready to go by morning. So we're all clear, this is for real? No take backs?"

"That's an odd way to put it," said Anna. "But yes. No take backs."

"Great. Bye." Daddy hit the End Call button, then turned the phone off. "Wiki, let's pack your stuff before they change their minds."

He jogged to the hall closet, grabbing the handle of a suitcase that was wedged in the back of the cramped space behind other stuff. He yanked with all his strength, causing the things in front of the suitcase—a stepladder, a box of Christmas decorations, an old lamp—to spill onto the floor. With the suitcase free, he didn't bother cleaning up the mess. He sprinted up the stairs, the newly freed luggage thumping each riser on the way.

"I don't want to go to Cosmos Camp, Mama." Wiki cut

her eyes to Leen, reading the hope and gratitude in her tics and tells. "This is Leen's thing."

Mama said, "Regardless of how it came to be, this is a great opportunity, girls."

Leen said, "It's not fair."

Wiki flinched.

Leen kept going, trying to soften her objection. "If she didn't really apply, that means someone else who actually applied couldn't get in. It's not Wiki's opportunity. It's someone else's."

Wiki squirmed at how insistent Leen was that she didn't belong at Cosmos Camp, but she still wanted out of it, so she said, "Cosmos Camp is expensive. That'll be hard when we're hiring farmhands for the summer, right?"

Mama's grin spread. Her eyes went wide and shiny. "Wrong. Before you came in, Anna explained the most generous part of the offer. Scholarships. For both of you! With your uncle Percy on the road and you two gone to Cosmos Camp, and now that we don't have to pay for it, your dad and I can hire more farmhands while you're away and relax a little for once!"

Overhead there was more thumping. Wiki imagined Daddy yanking the drawers from her dresser and upending the clothes into a rapidly filling suitcase.

Leen said, "But—"

"You're going. Both of you. End of conversation."

Above, a hard thump. Daddy shouted, "Ouch, my knee!"

Mama said, "I'm going to see if he needs help."

She ran upstairs with the nimble energy of an Olympian, leaving the sisters alone in a moment of awkward realization. Leen's frown was so extreme that it drove Wiki to make an uncharacteristic attempt at humor.

"The next Epic Ellisons adventure is about to begin, huh?"

Leen's shoulders slumped, and she trod upstairs. "I'm going to bed. See you in the morning. And every morning after that. Forever. I guess."

Since Wiki was the lone Ellison still downstairs, she didn't have to hide her hurt over being forced to go to Cosmos Camp *and* her sister not wanting her there.

The next morning, the three-hour drive from Logan County to the PeteyTech headquarters in Virginia Beach, Virginia, was quiet and awkward. Daddy slept in the passenger seat, having gotten up extra early to seal Leen's work shed with bricks and mortar. ("So nothing gets out while you're gone.") Mama drove while listening to *This Quirky Life*, her favorite podcast about the strange and unique things people all over the country experience. The new episode was about common, everyday stuff people see and remember differently for unexplained reasons. Like how some people remember

Thulu once being called Hulu, even though that was never a thing.

Leen had screwed in earbuds from the moment they left and hadn't spoken a word to Wiki. Wiki wouldn't force a chat, though Leen's attitude was generating less hurt and more anger the longer it went on. They were both getting summer circumstances they didn't want. So why was Leen acting like this was Wiki's fault?

But Wiki kept quiet and occupied herself through the ride reviewing every memory she had about PeteyTech and Cosmos Camp, whenever Mama's podcast wasn't distracting her.

Soothing Podcast Host: *—they aren't everywhere yet, so is it possible you're confusing hearing about them only recently with thinking they shouldn't exist? Because they do. Flying cars do exist.*

Frantic Podcast Guest Elaine Foster: *No. They aren't supposed to be here. Last summer they weren't there. At all. Now people are zipping around the sky like dragonflies. I'm telling you, something changed.*

Soothing Podcast Host: *Elaine Foster is currently a resident and patient at Sunnyview Mental Hospital in Upstate New York . . .*

Mama's podcasts were kinda creepy sometimes.

Wiki, unsettled for reasons beyond Elaine Foster's fate, focused on PeteyTech and Cosmos Camp.

Founded by Logan County native Petey Thunkle, Petey-Tech was the most innovative, most valuable, and most envied tech company on the planet. Of course, other companies tried to keep up by providing different and more affordable technology solutions. Like how their middle school got cheap computers from Artemis Microprocessors. Or how Ryder Communications Solutions provided subpar internet service to the neighboring county. PeteyTech's closest competitor, Whistleberry, made the most valiant effort in carving a name for themselves in the tech space, particularly with their cell phone offerings. But how could any company tussle with the kinds of innovations Petey Thunkle's brilliance produced?

Some people said every home on earth had a piece of PeteyTech in it, whether the residents knew it or not.

The company was always in the news, for better or worse. It seemed that anytime there was a new PeteyTech innovation, from supersmart ThunklePhones to, well, flying cars, there were tons of people waiting to sue Petey for stealing their ideas or warning of dire consequences for the environment, or whatever.

Daddy was a Petey Thunkle admirer and said people reacted so harshly to him because they didn't like change.

"Watch," Daddy liked to say, "that guy's going to be president one day!"

Mama was often more critical because she definitely didn't like change. "I miss being able to plug earbuds into my ThunklePhone. Now we gotta use those expensive Thunkle-Pod wireless things that look silly sticking out of your ears and are so easy to lose. If I ever get a word with Mr. Thunkle, Imma tell him a thing or two about that."

Despite all the controversies that Mama might want to tell Petey a thing or two about, Cosmos Camp was the one PeteyTech innovation that almost no one had a problem with. In its fifth year, the immersive program for young STEM—science, technology, engineering, and math—enthusiasts with an interest in space exploration was called "Geeky Gold" by *Time* magazine. *Wired*, a magazine Leen had had a subscription to ever since she learned to read, said Cosmos Camp graduates were destined to be the Next Great Minds in Human History.

Wiki thought that was putting a lot of pressure on kids going to a summer camp that was supposed to be about fun science, but Leen took it to heart. Her admiration of all things Thunkle was closer to Daddy's, while Wiki leaned toward Mama—particularly when it came to Cosmos Camp . . . or forcing *her* to come to Cosmos Camp. She might have a thing or two to say about that if she and Petey ever had a word.

The trees lining the highway thinned, and the sky widened the further east they drove. It wasn't superhot yet, so Mama rolled down the windows and Wiki tasted the sea salt in the air. She twisted away from her window, wondering if Leen was still grumpy and into her music, but the earbuds and ThunklePlayer rested between them. Leen seemed ready to stick her head out the window to get even nearer to the ocean. Or further away from Wiki.

Leen thought, *We're so close.*

Sure, she had been thrown a curveball last night with the "change in attendance" as she'd come to think about Wiki's invitation. Sure, it wasn't fair that something Leen had worked hard and planned for, for over two years, was handed to Wiki in a snap. But after listening to her favorite playlist and jotting a few ideas for new inventions in her ThunklePhone's Notepad app, she realized it didn't matter who else was at Cosmos Camp as long as she was.

Mama drove them to Atlantic Avenue. It was the last street before you hit the boardwalk, then the sand, then the ocean. They turned right, heading south, all of the Ellisons catching glimpses of diamondlike twinkles on the water in the gaps between hotels and restaurants. They got on a different road, then another road, and every new road saw the lively bustle of the beach give way to grass and sand dunes. Until . . .

"Oh my gosh!" Leen said, poking her head between the

front seats for a closer look, startling Daddy awake.

"What?" He swiped drool off his chin with the back of his hand. "What happened?"

A breathy Leen said, "PeteyTech."

They were still a mile or so away from the gate, but the facility was huge and impressive in a way that probably made it visible from orbit. The summer sun glinted off steel and polarized blue glass. The Rorrim Mirror Emporium back home had nothing on the hundreds of thousands of reflective panes that made up the campus's central structure: the Petey-Tech Tower skyscraper.

"Every window is also a solar panel," Leen said, "and the batteries that store the energy are in the support beams. Every part of the building powers every other part. Unlimited clean energy."

Wiki knew *that*, of course. Leen had been rattling off PeteyTech facts for months. But knowing and seeing weren't the same thing. Though Petey Thunkle's corporate headquarters might be the largest building Wiki had ever seen in real life, it wasn't the most impressive thing in their line of sight. Not by a longshot.

Miles beyond the gargantuan offices, closer to the ocean and towering in the sky, was something that looked suspiciously like a rocket ship.

Wiki pointed that way, startled. "Leen, what's that?"

Leen flopped back in her seat, her face twisted as if the question were an insult. "Ummm, the Interstellar-Z rocket."

It was mostly white with blue and red pinstriping, and letters that Wiki couldn't make out from this distance stenciled on the side. She'd seen rockets before, and this one was mostly similar to those—with the exception of a tip that was shaped something like a bird's beak instead of the conventional cone. So it wasn't the concept of a rocket that frightened Wiki, but this *specific* rocket. That it surprised her and her flawless memory. Maybe Leen hadn't mentioned it before?

Leen's face—her tics and tells—said otherwise. "Why are you acting like that, Wiki? I've been telling you about the Interstellar-Z for months. It's going on a moon mission in just a few weeks."

Wiki almost called Leen a liar . . . except that would've been rude and inaccurate. Leen's face showed no liar tics. Instead, she sat silently, and while Leen went back to gawking at all things PeteyTech, Wiki pinched a meaty part of her arm until it hurt. No, this wasn't one of the nightmares that concerned Leen so, the bad dreams where Wiki's most reliable gift—her memory—seemed to be malfunctioning. The dreams where she remembered things that never existed or forgot things that clearly existed.

Her bruising pinch did not ease her mind. Because dreams could be shaken off in the morning light.

This *was* morning though. She *wasn't* dreaming. Which meant something was very wrong.

If Leen had been telling her about that rocket and its trip to the moon for months, why did Wiki have no memory of those conversations whatsoever?

3
Petey Thunkle Is WHAT?!

Mama showed a jolly security guard at the PeteyTech gate the Cosmos Camp forms for the girls, then they were directed to a parking lot to the right of the gleaming glass-and-steel tower at the center of the campus, where they were to unload their belongings and register with the staff. Even if the guard hadn't given them detailed directions, they couldn't miss the swaying banners set up at strategic intervals, declaring phrases like "You're Only 100 Yards from Liftoff" and "Your Initial Ascent Starts Around the Corner." Leen vibrated with excitement as Mama pulled the car up with the other arrivals.

They were in a line before a massive building with big bay doors as tall as apartment buildings in the front. Leen had seen airplane hangars before, on TV and such. None this big, though. She realized it was likely designed to emulate elongated hangars meant for housing narrow rockets the height of buildings. The sign over the doors read "Cosmos Camp Training Facility and Space Museum."

There were smaller, people-sized doors adjacent to the bay doors and, outside, a long table where PeteyTech employees helped register the arriving campers.

"Well, girls, this is it!" Daddy squealed.

Before Mama could shift the car into park, Daddy hopped out, popped the trunk, and began dumping Wiki's and Leen's bags on the sidewalk. Leen exited, as did Mama, but Wiki was a bit slower, her attention still on the huge rocket east of them.

Daddy knocked on her window. "Y'all know if we need to sign something before we hit the road?"

He backed up enough so Wiki could actually get out of the car. Leen tugged on her backpack and grabbed her suitcase. Wiki joined her, doing the same. They'd have to carry the trunk containing some of their shared belongings—including some Epic Ellisons goodies they were never without—between them. They each took a handle and hoisted the heavy chest with visible effort.

"Hey, do you two need some help?" asked a gangly boy with braces, dark brown skin, and black hair that was curly *and* shiny.

Wiki said, "I think we're okay, but thank—"

A gushing Leen released her handle, letting her side of the trunk THUNK hard on the sidewalk. "We sure could use a hand."

Wiki groaned and wondered if Sheed Alston suddenly felt a chill go up his spine back home in Logan County.

Eager to fulfill his offer of assistance, the curly-haired boy rushed to Leen's aid, hoisting the entire trunk onto his shoulder in a feat of strength that defied his beanpole frame.

Wiki said, "Be careful not to hurt yourself!"

"Oh, no worries. I lifted with my legs. Using larger muscle fibers in my quadriceps instead of hinging my lower back reduces the chance for initial injury. After that, it's only a matter of balancing the load."

Leen slow blinked, trying not to swoon. "What is your name?"

"I'm Kelvin!"

"Leen!" She pointed at herself, then, with less enthusiasm, said, "That's my sister, Wiki."

"Greetings," Wiki said, tired of this whole thing already.

"Do you have your cabin assignment yet?"

The girls shook their heads. Leen said, "I think Mama and Daddy have to check us in."

Daddy quick stepped from the registration table with a couple of thick folders and Cosmos Camp IDs dangling from lanyards. When he spotted the girls, he jogged over. "These are your camp badges"—he shoved the lanyards at them—"and your welcome packets." He wedged the folders into the crook of Wiki's elbow. "We signed all the waivers and put money in your Camp Wallets so you'll only need to call in case of emergencies."

Mama joined him, looking annoyed. "You don't have to sound this eager."

"Oh yes I do," Daddy said.

Leen motioned to their new helper. "Daddy, this is Kelvin."

"Hey, boy," Daddy said, barely sparing a second to look at Kelvin. To the girls he said, "Y'all good?"

Wiki, reading their father like a book, gave the man the thing he most desired. "We're good, Daddy. You can leave now."

He kissed each girl on the forehead. "Love you, and love you too."

As soon as Mama got her hugs and kisses, Daddy scooped her up like in those old photos from the day they got married, hurled her into the passenger seat, then slid across the hood to reach the driver's side and slip behind the wheel, not even bothering to adjust the seat their much-shorter mother had been in, so his knees were to his chin, probably suffering friction burns from the way he whipped the wheel like a NASCAR driver racing from the PeteyTech lot.

Kelvin said, "He sure was in a hurry."

He's the only one, Wiki thought. Accepting her unfair and unexpected fate, Wiki slipped the lanyard over her head, not even bothering to read the information on her camp credentials, then checked the paperwork Daddy had shoved her way. "We're Cabin 1A."

Leen, perky the way she always was when a cute boy was in the vicinity, snapped off a salute and said, "Kelvin, lead the way."

In 1A, along with two bundles of Cosmos Camp swag, which included their camp uniforms/jumpsuits, were instructions to meet in the training area at 14:00 hours (2:00 p.m., Wiki's brain instantly calculated) for camp orientation.

Leen had warmed up a bit since Kelvin had dropped their belongings at their door. She was finally *here*. Among the smartest twelve-year-olds around. Where she belonged!

And so was Wiki.

That wasn't necessarily a bad thing, she told herself. Just . . . *unexpected*! So she'd had an unexpected reaction—rage!—to the news. That's all. She was over it. Completely. She would prove it by engaging her beloved twin sister in conversation. Leen said, "Hey."

Wiki barely glanced up from the camp pamphlets she was committing to memory. "Hey."

All righty then.

"It is my job," the absolutely *regal* Black woman at the podium said drolly, "to welcome you, the greatest young scientific minds from across the country, to the fifth annual PeteyTech Cosmos Camp, where you'll learn all about the various roles and research required for space exploration before going on your own, simulated, space mission. My name is Dr. Antoinette Burr, and I, along with my assistants, Sam and Ralph, will be your Cosmos Camp mentors for the duration of your stay."

Dr. Burr had the plainest Cosmos Camp jumpsuit in the room—gray—but it was offset by her beautifully glowing dark brown skin, gorgeous hoop earrings, and immaculate shoulder-length black braids decorated with seashell beads and golden silk strands. Leen made a mental note to convince Mama to let her wear braids like Dr. Burr's as her back-to-school hairstyle.

Blaring pep-rally music echoed around the massive training facility, and the assistants flanking the stage danced enthusiastically. Their movements were high energy and goofy. One did a somersault. This was all the more impressive because Dr. Burr's assistants were robots.

They were about five feet tall, with gleaming shells—one red, one blue—covering everything but their joints, making them look like a cross between a person and the classic cars Mr. Green back home loved to drive around town. Their heads were dome shaped, and their "faces" were digital

29

displays currently lit with happy-face emojis. Their movements were so nimble and fluid. One dropped into a split, then popped into the air for a toe touch. The other observed, his posture suggesting he sensed a challenge, then dropped into a break-dancer's hurricane spin. Leen very much wanted to take one of those robots apart to see how they worked.

Most of the room ran up to the stage and clapped to the robotic dance battle. Though Wiki seemed unimpressed, and that irked Leen.

Didn't Wiki know that Dr. Antoinette Burr was a noted engineer, designer, and inventor who shunned other fancier jobs because she believed in the good work PeteyTech did to change the world? Rude.

Wiki, of course, didn't mean to be rude. The robots were neat, she guessed, but were they really that impressive? Not to her. Not when PeteyTech had, like, a gazillion dollars and Leen once made her own impressive—though somewhat unhinged—robot from Logan County junk. Robot aesthetics was a back-of-her-mind concern; her primary attention was on the high windows to the far left of the hangar.

Through them, the Interstellar-Z rocket was visible, and Wiki still couldn't shake her unease over having no memory of the spacecraft until that morning. When Leen lightly elbowed her in the ribs, she snapped back to the present. Annoyed.

"Pay attention," Leen whisper-yelled.

The robots had frozen in their final dance poses, and the music cut out. Some of the campers continued to chatter and clap, but Dr. Burr motioned to their seats. "Settle down, settle down. There's more."

There were eight campers total, divided among three rows. The girls were in the back row with their across-the-hall neighbors from Cabin 2A—Sierra Ramos from Brooklyn, New York, and Britney McGill from Des Moines, Iowa. Their morning helper, Kelvin, somehow seeming ganglier, was in the front row, though he twisted to wave at Wiki and Leen when everyone was seated.

Dr. Burr continued with little enthusiasm. "As you know, PeteyTech is the world's greatest innovator of state-of-the-art, well, everything. Though I think it's best you heard about it directly from the man himself." Somehow her voice became even less enthusiastic. "Please welcome . . . Petey Thunkle!"

Everyone stood again, buzzing with anticipation.

The applause stretched, then thinned, then died when Petey Thunkle did not take the podium.

"Oh, I forgot something," Dr. Burr said in a tone that reminded Wiki of a time a boy in the school play forgot his lines and ended up reading them, emotionless, off note cards. "Look under your chairs."

Everyone did as told. Wiki and Leen freed slim boxes from beneath their seats. Exchanging perplexed looks, they popped the box tops and found sleek sets of . . .

"VR goggles," Leen said, impressed. She'd been building her own versions of such goggles for the better part of the year.

Dr. Burr said, "Everyone put on your headsets and power up."

When Wiki had her goggles firmly affixed, she pressed the Power button near the right temple and the world shifted.

There was the sense of traveling through a tunnel of misty blue and turquoise light with the sound of wind whooshing through the headset's speakers before the pixels rearranged into twelve seats before a podium, all floating through the void of space.

Well, not a void . . . That was clearly Saturn off to their left. The campers gasped.

Ahead of them, at the podium, Dr. Burr was no longer alone.

Petey Thunkle, dressed in his signature jeans, hoodie, and suit coat, greeted them all with a hearty wave, then flickered away like a glitch in a video game. The outline of his body remained visible, but all the details inside were replaced by a mix of numbers and characters that made up whatever code ran the simulation they were viewing. As quick as they'd gone, the details of Petey's features reappeared. "Hey, everybody! I'm sorry to give you prerecorded avatar me, but the life of a tech company CEO is a busy one. Something some of you will undoubtedly experience yourself one day."

A girl in the middle row, who sat among two other campers Wiki and Leen hadn't met yet, groaned and worked on her manicure with a nail file. *Odd*, Wiki thought.

Prerecorded avatar Petey kept talking. "Cosmos Camp isn't just about space exploration. Though that is humanity's next frontier, the lessons you learn here will help you conquer whatever challenges you face in the fields of engineering, physics, computer programming, business, market—*zzzzz, zzzzz*—"

Wiki's head tilted. Leen leaned forward.

Petey's audio went from staticky to completely mute. The avatar's lips moved, it made expressive gestures with its hands, but there was no sound.

Leen tapped her goggles lightly. Wiki was about to raise her hand to alert someone when another avatar stepped from behind Petey as if she'd come through a hidden door.

It was Anna Thunkle in a breezy, flower-print dress, waddling into view.

Her swollen tummy stuck out a good six inches from the rest of her. As Mama would say whenever she spotted a very pregnant neighbor around town, "She is with child, and that child is lounging."Anna looked a mix of elated and panicked. She spoke rapidly, rubbing her belly the whole time. "Victoria and Evangeleen, if you can see and hear me, please don't say nothing. This message is meant for y'all and y'all only."

Leen's hand found its way to Wiki's knee and squeezed. Wiki's hand fell on top of Leen's and squeezed back.

"Tonight, when a moment presents itself, please sneak from your cabins and make your way to the main tower, floor forty-four. You will, unfortunately, have to use your wits to skirt around the various security measures in place. I wish I had time to explain further, but that is not the case right now. If what our research says about the two of you is true, then I'm certain what is required is within your skill set. Once you've reached my floor, everything will be made clear. There's so much to explain but know this: my sweetie Petey went missing a week ago, and we need you to find him. Keep this in the strictest confidence—that's something else my research says shouldn't be an issue for you. I'll see you tonight."

Anna stepped behind the Petey avatar again and vanished.

Petey's audio returned. "—*zzzzz, zzzzz*—look up at all those stars in the sky and know you're on track to be among them!"

More cheers from all the campers who'd heard Petey's uninterrupted motivational speech. But with what the Epic Ellisons had just heard—

My sweetie Petey went missing a week ago, and we need you to find him.

—neither Wiki nor Leen saw this as a clap-worthy moment.

4

A Chill(y) Reception

After orientation concluded and everyone deposited their VR headsets in special receptacles at the front of the room, Dr. Burr initiated an "icebreaker," where all the campers got to meet the training robots and each other. Wiki and Leen were slow to part, both stunned by what they—and nobody else, apparently—had seen and heard from Anna Thunkle.

"We can't talk about it here," Wiki said, knowing that part of being able to sneak to the forty-fourth floor that night meant not raising any suspicions now. Anyone could be watching, and Wiki could not shake the feeling that someone *was*. It was a tickle at the back of her neck, an uneasy churn in her stomach. Though a quick scan of the room didn't out any obvious spies.

"I know that," Leen said, displeased that even more Epic Ellisons stuff was intruding on her camp experience.

Dr. Burr had told the group this was a time to "present your best you" and "make friends that would last a lifetime." Intimidating tasks on normal days—what if your best you wasn't good enough?

Now that Leen knew the CEO of the gosh-dang company was missing and they might have to find him, it was even harder to concentrate on being the best her.

Focus, focus. "I'm going to mingle."

She left Wiki and approached a loose group of campers who'd been in the row ahead of them during Dr. Burr's welcome speech. She extended her hand, like Mama taught her. "Hi, I'm Evangeleen Ellison from Logan County, Virginia."

The three campers, who hadn't been talking as much as evaluating the room, reacted coldly to her greeting. So much so that she lowered her hand after awkward seconds of it hovering between them.

A short boy with broad shoulders and puffy hands like bear claws (the pastry, not actual bear claws), said, "I avoid all skin-to-skin contact whenever possible. Germs."

"Oh, right," Leen said, realizing that was reasonable. You definitely shouldn't touch people, or pressure them to touch you if you or they don't want to be touched. Germs or not!

He jerked his chin at her. "Pierre Dunston. Los Angeles, California."

"Nice to meet you, Pierre," Leen said.

Pierre did not indicate he felt the same.

The pale, pencil-thin girl with black hair, blue lipstick (that was kinda cool—Mama didn't even let them *think about* makeup yet), and dangly skull earrings, who'd been working on her nails during Petey's speech, snatched Leen's hand and squeezed hard. "I'm Harlow Garrison of Kissimmee, Florida."

Leen tried not to wince. "Hey, Harlow."

The third kid was *big*. Like he could be the quarterback on Daddy's favorite football team big. Leen might've confused him for a PeteyTech employee if he hadn't been in an oversized camper jumpsuit. He was blond and tanned, with shoulders that were wide in a way that made Leen think he could be made of brick. He gently pried Leen's hand from Harlow's, bent at the waist, and kissed Leen's knuckles. "I'm Chest Channing, of the Westport Channings."

"Chest?" Leen said aloud, not meaning to. She managed to keep her follow-up question— *Are you thirty?*—to herself.

"Short for Chester. Of the Westport Channings."

"You said that part already." His huge hand was yucky damp. Leen wriggled free and wiped her palm on her jumpsuit.

"You know, you should smile more," Chest said.

Leen *was* smiling until he said that. Then they all stared at each other. Leen's gaze pinging between Pierre, Harlow, and Chest. She struggled with a polite way to end the encounter— maybe they'd get to know one another better once camp activities began.

Harlow broke the awkward silence. "What's your specialty?"

"Specialty?" Leen tried to remember if that was something she had to state on her application. "I like making stuff. One time, I made a robot to play tag with, but it went a little bonkers."

She trailed off on the last word because Harlow glanced at Pierre, did a weird smirk, then Pierre's eyes crinkled in a funny way and Leen couldn't read faces the way Wiki could but something in it felt mean. Chest was flexing his arm and admiring his own bulging bicep.

Leen fought to not stare at the floor.

Harlow said, "I'm partial to physics. Thermodynamics, in particular. I published my first paper in the *Advanced Scientific Journal for Kids* when I was, oh, seven."

Pierre jumped in. "It's engineering for me. Emphasis on hydraulics with some interest in aqueducts, spillways, and dams. I'm interested in controlling how people get water one day."

"You want to help people get water?" Leen said, thinking that sounded cool.

"Did I say 'help'?" Pierre posited.

Chest spoke before Leen could think about that too hard. "I'm interested in quantum computing but dabble a bit in electromagnetism. I'm weird that way."

"Oh." The disciplines they referenced weren't unfamiliar to

Leen. The way they expressed them made Leen self-conscious. She just didn't think about *specialties* when she made things back home. Should she?

Harlow heavily sighed. "It looks like we've confused her. Here's an easier question: What device are you carrying?"

"Device?"

"Your. Phone."

"Oh. Right. It's the new ThunklePhone. It was a gift from—"

She almost said her hometown, Fry, but that might require more of an explanation than she wanted to give. She and Wiki had received phones from the mayor's office because of their last big save-the-town adventure. Leen didn't want to get into any details about being an Epic Ellison. She just wanted to be Leen here. Maybe figure out her specialty.

She coughed in her fist and said, "It was just a gift."

"It's trash," Harlow said and produced her own phone. "The new Whistleberry is superior in every way. Camera. Audio. Screen resolution. Isn't that right?"

The question was directed to Pierre and Chest, who scrambled to pull out their own Whistleberry phones.

Leen said, "They do seem nice."

"Just an FYI. If you're looking for something you can easily improve."

The phones were the only things about these three that seemed nice.

"It was a pleasure to meet you," Leen lied before scampering away.

Across the room near a bowl filled with some cool purple punch, Wiki spoke fast, her drink swishing around the plastic cup in her hand while Kelvin, Sierra, and Britney nodded along with captivated smiles. Leen slunk that way slowly, catching Wiki midstory.

"—we deduced they were hiding the farmer's market money they stole in fake loaves of bread! It was really wild and—oh, oh, Leen. Come here."

Leen came closer, her guard up.

Wiki said, "I was telling them about that time, at the farmer's market, when those thieves stole the Pepperlings' money and we used one of our robots to figure out who—"

"Mine," Leen said.

Wiki stopped talking, confused.

Leen, feeling just . . . grouchy, finally figured out what she should've said to Harlow, Pierre, and Chest. "Robots are *my* specialty."

"Sure," said Wiki, "you're really good at making robots."

Leen addressed not just Wiki but Kelvin, Sierra, and Britney too, so everyone was clear on this. "You help sell my robots at the farmer's market, but I build them. Without any help. Okay."

Wiki's lips puckered. She sat her cup on the table, no longer thirsty or very talkative. "I'm glad you cleared that up for everybody, sis. I'll see you in our cabin."

Wiki nodded to their campmates, then walked away, leaving Leen feeling like, perhaps, she shouldn't have said what she'd said the way she said it.

Sierra and Britney gave Leen wary looks and said they'd see her tomorrow, but it was the way people say it when they aren't looking forward to it. They went to explore other corners of the icebreaker party, leaving Leen alone with Kelvin.

Without a hint of sarcasm or meanness, he said, "I think we're all going to be best friends forever. Don't you?"

When it came to reading faces and signals and general vibes, Leen figured Kelvin might be the worst of them all.

Leen spent another hour hovering around group conversations that didn't include her, then an hour after that staring at the last few years of Cosmos Camp group photos. In the original Cosmos Camp class from four years ago were two kids who'd skipped high school altogether to study aerospace engineering at the best college in the country. In the camp photo from three years ago was a person who invented a machine that converted scorched earth into something like super fertilizer, giving forests that had been damaged by wildfires a turbo boost on the regrowing process. Last year's camp class had four kids who'd teamed up to develop a new sort of wing that could revolutionize air travel, making planes not just faster but more ecofriendly due to increased fuel efficiency. Inspiration and innovation thrived at Cosmos Camp, and that's what Leen was going to focus on more than anything! So they'd have to resolve this Petey Thunkle situation ASAP. Leen needed to rest her brain for tomorrow.

The icebreaker party ended, and campers were instructed to return to their quarters for a good night's rest. Tomorrow would be busy!

Leen returned to her bunk and found Wiki already there. Her camp jumpsuit was folded neatly at the foot of her bed, replaced by a black-on-black outfit. Sneaking clothes.

All Wiki said was "Ready when you are."

Wiki was mad-mad, and Leen didn't have to read any tics or tells to know it. When you've been around someone your whole life and longer, the emotions they hide from the world can seem as bright as neon signs. Part of Leen wanted to apologize, but a bigger part didn't. And an apology didn't mean anything if it wasn't coming from all of you.

"Give me five minutes," Leen said. She got dressed, geared up, grabbing her trusty sneak bag—an Epic Ellisons essential—and wondered if all of her would be ready for that apology in the morning.

5

Elevators Are Way Cooler on the Inside

Dressed in all black, Wiki and Leen slipped from their bunk as fluidly as ink en route to Anna Thunkle's floor.

Wiki, still very irritated with Leen but focused on the mission, said, "I left the party early to get a better sense of the building layout, so listen up . . ."

On Wiki's instructions, they cleared the cabin corridors, slipped by a common area where Britney was playing Chest in a heated game of checkers, and disabled a security camera with one of Leen's sticky loopers—devices that looked like mini hockey pucks but stuck to anything you threw them at. Tossed anywhere near a security camera, they overrode the live feed and created a video loop so anyone watching only saw an empty hallway.

That got them out of the training hangar. Now came the hard part.

A long corridor connected the hangar to PeteyTech Tower, and that path had way more cameras than the girls had sticky loopers. Going outside and around the atrium presented a similar camera-quantity issue with the added obstacle of patrolling security guards. Which left one other option.

The roof.

Where the two structures met was a ventilation system situated high on the wall. Leen boosted Wiki, who pried the cover open, then shimmied in before tossing back a length of rope that Leen climbed. They spent the next twenty minutes scooting through the dusty aluminum conduit until they found a fork that went left, right, and up. Rungs set in the side of the vertical conduit took them to a ceiling hatch that Wiki cut open with a mini welding torch of Leen's design.

Emerging from the dusty vent, Leen sneezed a bunch of times and Wiki didn't say "bless you" once, so . . . still angry.

The roof gave them a clear path to the main tower, and once there, they only needed to pick the lock on the elevator maintenance door to access the shaft, with its cars traveling up and down. The next problem: it was pretty hard to get into an elevator car from inside the shaft.

"Three . . ." Wiki said.

"Two . . ." said Leen.

"One!" they said together, leaping into empty air for a split second before a fast-traveling elevator car shot up to meet them.

Leen tugged down the goggles resting atop her head, then tapped a command into the control gauntlet on her wrist. Information about the elevator's programming appeared in her Heads-Up Display.

"Can you take control?" Wiki asked.

Leen scoffed, then took over. "The forty-third floor should do it."

The car stopped at the floor below their forty-fourth-floor destination, putting them at eye level to where they were trying to go. Another gauntlet command opened the door, and Wiki leapt up onto forty-four.

When Leen took control of their forty-fourth-floor door, she lost control of the elevator. At that moment, someone, somewhere in the building called the car they'd rode to a lower floor. In the moment before the car zipped down, Leen jumped. Wiki, flat on her stomach, her arm extended into the shaft, caught Leen by the wrist. With their ride already ten floors below and descending fast. Leen dangled over a dark and terrifying drop.

"I've got you," Wiki assured Leen, bracing herself.

"I know." Leen planted her feet inside the shaft and climbed her sister's arm.

A final heaving effort got Leen on solid ground, and the door to the elevator shaft dinged shut while they lay on the floor panting. They were breathing so hard they barely noticed the whirring motor approaching.

They sat up and watched the tiny, disc-shaped machine make its way toward them. It was one of those Thoomba robots that automatically cleans floors.

Last year's hottest holiday gift! Wiki recalled multiple advertisements, and the fluffy news stories Mama watched in the mornings bloomed in her head like an explosion. This sudden rush of memory caused a mild headache. In the midst of that new and throbbing pain was a strange, nonsensical word that she wanted to dismiss but was unable to because her memory never let her dismiss anything. So instead, the ridiculous word grew into a question: *What the heck is a* Roomba?

"Wiki!" Leen snapped her fingers an inch from Wiki's nose. "You're glitching again!"

That was Leen's term for when Wiki got so lost in her vast memory bank that she zoned out, like a trance. From Leen's perspective, her sister's computer brain was glitching the same way regular computers sometimes do.

Wiki shook her head, jarring herself back into the moment. "I'm fine. I'm here."

Leen's attention jumped from her sister to the finer details of this particular Thoomba. It was shinier than the home models people bought from the Thunkle-Mart or online from Thunkle-Zon. It looked silver or maybe even platinum, but Leen bet that would've made it too heavy—and expensive—to be a robot made for a single household chore.

Then a second, smaller disc—a lens—inset atop the

robot projected a spectrum of rainbow colors. A hazy, translucent hologram of a prim and proper woman formed in the air. Most of a woman. She didn't have legs.

Everything from the waist down swirled into a cone of light, like the smoky bottom half of a genie tethered to its lamp. She had a white blouse, a freshly bobbed haircut, and horn-rimmed glasses. She said, "Hello, girls. I'm Pettygrew, Anna Thunkle's virtual assistant."

Even though her head projected to the height of approximately five foot seven, when she spoke, her voice came from floor level, a speaker built into the device, which was a little hard to hear because the Thoomba was still vacuuming.

"Would you mind turning off your motor?" Wiki asked.

Pettygrew glanced down, then shook her head, embarrassed. The vacuum motor cut off. "Pardon me, I tend to multitask."

Leen circled the assistant, guessing at how she functioned. The hologram seemed happy to have her attention. "You'd like to know what I do, huh?"

"Sure," Leen said.

"My programming is beyond extensive. I speak every known language—very useful for international business calls. I have access to most known historical texts, from Shakespeare to how to properly spear a fish. I know the complete works of every notable philosopher, inventor, scientist, and mathematician. I've read every comic book ever printed. I'm very well-rounded."

Leen whistled. "You sound amazing!"

"Oh, I am."

Wiki was impressed but also impatient. They'd gone through a lot to get here, let's get on with it. "What's next, Pettygrew?"

"Yes. Of course. As I was saying, I work for Anna Thunkle and will take you to her now. Please, this way."

The Thoomba and its holographic AI reversed course, zooming down the corridor it had come from. The girls followed.

The forty-fourth floor offered what was likely a stunning

view of Virginia Beach in daytime. On a cloudy and moonless night like this, when the only visible part of the ocean were the whitecaps crashing against dark sand, and scattered lights from the boardwalk hotels stood in for the stars, it was way creepy. Pettygrew took them around a corner, changing the view drastically. Now, in the distance, was the massive Interstellar-Z rocket and the scaffolding surrounding it as crews upon crews worked on the day and night preparations that would see it launch in just a few weeks. Wiki's unease (and headache) doubled at the sight of that rocket.

Another turn at the end of yet another long corridor had Pettygrew stop, then spin to face them. She motioned to a set of polished doors. Leen turned the knob, since Pettygrew's hologram hands couldn't, and the assistant said, "Welcome to Anna's suite."

The room before them was so wide and spacious it made the furniture look small, even though it was really big. A big couch and TV took up one section of the floor. A big kitchen area at another section. No walls separated the areas, the boundaries set merely by how each section was arranged with wide gaps of concrete floor between them. The section that drew, and kept, the girls' attention was the big desk that Anna Thunkle lay upon. People didn't usually lie down on desks, and the way she pressed at her bulging stomach and grimaced sent Wiki and Leen racing to her, panicked.

"Anna!" Wiki yelled.

"Are you all right?" Leen asked.

Anna turned her anguished face toward the girls. And burped. Loud.

Wiki and Leen skidded to a stop while Anna's face smoothed into relieved ecstasy. She righted herself, sitting so her legs hung over the front edge of the desk. "Excuse me, girls. It's just when you're this far along with child, you can be very gassy and baby *does not like that*." She spoke directly to her belly. "Isn't that right, little one?"

Pettygrew motored next to Wiki and Leen. "The Epic Ellisons, as requested."

"Yes, yes. Thank you, Pettygrew. That'll be all for now. I think a maintenance bot made a mess upstairs in the residence—a lot of dust and you know how I sneeze. Could you take care of that before retiring for the night?"

"Certainly," said Pettygrew. Her vacuum motor revved and she zipped from the room.

"Thank you for coming—and in such spectacular fashion," said Anna, gingerly lowering her bare feet to the floor. She penguin-waddled around the desk to the high-backed chair on the opposite side. "I observed your daring work in the elevator shaft and you are everything Pettygrew's research indicated. Definitely who my Petey wanted to bring him home."

Wiki's face scrunched. "About that. You said he was missing? Like, how?"

"Was he kidnapped?" Leen said with more hopeful glee than everyone else was comfortable with.

The girls waited, but Anna was back to rubbing her belly and looking like she was in agony. She burped again, then resumed her explanation. "Whew . . . I think that's Baby Thunkle saying it's a little more complicated than that. Come. I'll show you!"

Anna typed a command into her desktop keyboard, and the bookshelves on the far right of the suite slid aside, revealing a hidden door. She keyed in another command, and the door swung open slowly with the sound of hissing air. The corridor beyond was dark, and a breeze significantly colder than the already-cool air-conditioning wafted toward them.

Anna waddled to a coatrack by the office entrance, grabbed a heavy, fur-lined parka and a pair of smaller, heavily insulated coats that she brought to the girls.

"Pettygrew says these should fit."

Wiki and Leen put them on, while Anna shrugged into hers on her way toward the frigid tunnel. "You've seen my office. Now it's time you saw Petey's. Don't worry. We probably won't stay long enough for frostbite to set in."

6

What Came First?

The farther along the tunnel went, the colder it got. Wiki's and Leen's teeth were chattering by the time they reached yet another sealed door that Anna punched yet another code into before they could enter.

Beyond, it got significantly colder and significantly weirder.

They were now in a massive, egg-shaped room that had to occupy at least ten stories' worth of space in the very center of the PeteyTech skyscraper. The tunnel led them onto a catwalk-like platform that ran along the perimeter and crisscrossed to a large computer bank; desks, couches, and other office stuff were suspended in the center of the steel-mesh platform like a fly in a spider's web. The curved ceiling stretched way over their heads into near darkness, and the curved floor extended a couple of stories down, though the smooth bottom was visible.

"What is this?" Leen asked, questioning the logic of such an oddly engineered space.

Anna said, "Petey called this room 'the Egg.' And the office setup in the center is 'the Chicken.'"

"Why?" Leen asked.

"It's a joke based on the shape of the room, isn't it? Because of the old"—Wiki winced and massaged her temple, her head pounding—"dilemma. What came first: the chicken or the egg?"

Anna beamed. "Exactly."

They took one of the six, crisscrossing catwalk paths leading to the center work area, which was mounted on a thick, stainless-steel column. Leen noted how perfectly smooth the inside of the Egg's walls seemed. What was it made of? Fiberglass? Some new kind of polymer?

Wiki couldn't care less about what the room was made of. Her headache worsened by the second, and she gripped the safety rail tightly because her legs were starting to feel like cooked spaghetti.

They reached the vast work area, which was surprisingly neat, save for some uneven flooring. Anna led the way and warned them to watch their step around the various floor grooves. "Easy to trip," she noted.

The computer monitors were powered down. With the exception of a coffee mug filled with a variety of pens, the desk was clutter-free. The only odd thing . . . clothing folded neatly on the chair Wiki and Leen presumed belonged to Petey.

Leen tugged her goggles on and snapped photos. "This what he was wearing the last time you saw him?"

"Yes," said Anna.

A dark-blue cardigan sweater. A knit cap. Scarf. Gloves. A heavy coat.

All the cold-weather gear needed to work comfortably in such a frigid space. Yet no Petey. Not even a frozen one.

Despite the throbbing in her skull, Wiki craned her neck, searching the high curve of the Egg. "No cameras in here, huh?"

"Petey wouldn't allow it."

Leen asked, "Why's it so cold?"

"Petey adhered to several studies that claimed humans processed information better in lower temperatures. This was where he did his best thinking, came up with his most innovative ideas, so I suppose there's something to that theory."

"When did you know something was wrong?" the girls asked in unison.

Anna flinched from surprise, then answered. "Whenever he came in here for one of his marathon brainstorming sessions, he told me to check on him if he wasn't back in twenty-four hours. I never had to before. But last week he went over his time and was due in an important meeting with the government about the Interstellar-Z launch. When I came to check on him, I found this note!"

Anna produced a folded slip of paper and presented it to the girls. It read:

Anna, My Bae,

> *If you're reading this, then I have missed my twenty-four-hour window and that's way longer than I intended. I can't be more specific about what I was working on or how I was working on it in case this message should ever fall into the wrong hands, but I trust you, sweet sugarplum, to decipher what and who is needed here. You know where we grew up. You remember how strange it could be there. Well, there's a pair of genius problem-solvers there who can help. They're the best at what they do. Find them. They can bring me home. Until we're reunited, your forever love ~P.T.*

Wiki, having committed the letter to memory, refolded it and returned it to Anna. "How long since he missed his window?"

"Three days."

"So that's why you wanted Wiki to come?" Leen said somewhat excitedly. "Not because you thought she really belonged at Cosmos Camp?"

Wiki gave Leen a scolding look worthy of their mama.

Anna's attention bounced between the two of them. "Oh dear. I wouldn't put it that way. It's been a long time since I left Logan County. When Petey mentioned a pair of geniuses from back home, I put Pettygrew on the job, and her research found you two almost instantly. When she informed me that one of you was already attending Cosmos Camp, it seemed like a lucky break in an unlucky week."

Wiki put her irritation with Leen aside. "Something else happened? Not just Petey going missing?"

Anna pursed her lips, clearly considering how much more she should say.

Wiki said, "This is the richest company in the world. Don't you have security that's, like, grown-up? Just because Petey wanted us to do something doesn't mean we have to do it. Mama says we should make sure folks respect our time and energy."

Anna rubbed her belly. "Everything I'm telling you is a pinkie-swear secret. Okay?" She offered her pinkie.

Wiki sighed but gave in and hooked Anna's finger with hers. Anna repeated the gesture with Leen.

Anna said, "Someone's been messing with the Interstellar-Z,

making unexplained alterations to the navigation program that we'd miss if not for our daily safety checks."

Leen gasped. "Sabotage?" The thought of someone messing up a perfectly good rocket saddened her so.

"We don't use the s-word around here. Especially in front of our board of directors. Or investors. Or marketing department. Or—"

Wiki said, "We get it. You want to keep it a secret from a lot of important people. Because of money, I guess."

The girls had firsthand knowledge of how much money influenced adults'—sometimes very bad—decisions. This felt like one of those times.

"Not just money, no. Competition and prestige. There are many people who'd love to see PeteyTech fail even once. Corporate rivals like Artemis Microprocessors or Ryder Communications Solutions or our biggest competitor, Whistleberry. We cannot seem weak or vulnerable."

Anna's brow furrowed and her lips pinched. "You don't have to look at me like that. This is Petey's company, and his wishes. He wants the launch to go smoothly because that will make all sorts of life-changing innovations possible. More people will trust PeteyTech, which will allow PeteyTech to create more things people trust!"

Wiki recognized that "trust" line from a PeteyTech ad that aired three and half years ago.

Leen spun slowly in place, taking scans of the Chicken's workstation and the Egg's walls with her goggles. "So, get Petey back—that's the assignment."

"Getting him back's the most important thing." Anna smiled wide again. "Anything else you want to look into is icing on the cake."

Wiki's eyes narrowed. "You want us to find the saboteur too."

"We don't like to use that s-word either. But yes. That would also be helpful. We've had trouble in the past with corporate spies trying to steal our secrets or worse. Ryder Communications had a mole in our research-and-development department for a time. The Artemis people tried to hack us. We stopped them before any real damage was done, but we know they keep trying."

Wiki said, "I can understand why that concerns *you*. But you still haven't said why it should concern *us*. Mama also says 'genius' don't mean 'free.'"

"Wik!" Leen said. *How rude.*

"No, no," Anna said, "you're right. I'm asking you to do a job, and people get stuff for doing jobs. How do college scholarships, guaranteed internships, and a lucrative employment offer when you're grown-up sound?"

The girls were stunned silent.

The number-one phrase around the Ellisons' house was

"money don't grow on trees." Already Mama and Daddy had prepared them for how expensive things were, and in those conversations, college—especially for *two girls* going at the same time—came up plenty. They'd stressed that the girls use their smarts to try and get their education paid for through grants and scholarships, and here comes Anna Thunkle, offering solutions for a job well done.

The girls exchanged looks, communicating in a way they'd been capable of since birth, considering the offer.

Perhaps they were taking too long, though. Because Anna sweetened the deal in a super distressing way.

"I understand I'm likely underestimating your talents here," Anna said, "so what if PeteyTech offered to save your family farm?"

Wiki cocked her head.

Leen sucked a sharp, whistling breath through her teeth.

Together, they said, "What do you mean 'save'?"

Anna pressed a hand to her mouth. "Oh my. I thought— I *assumed* you knew. I—"

But Wiki was already stomping to the far side of the Egg, thumbing a text message to the family group chat.

Wiki

Are we in danger of losing the farm?

What? Why are you asking that? You're supposed to be focused on camp.

Is it true?

Stay out of grown folks' business, Victoria! Now, unless there's something wrong with you or your sister, have a good night.

Leen, who'd been monitoring the conversation on her own phone, looked up and said, "Daddy wants us to stay out of grown folks' business and he used your full name."

Wiki met her eyes. "So it is true."

The girls sighed in unison. Shook their heads in unison. Then, they addressed Anna Thunkle: "The Epic Ellisons got you covered. We're in."

7

Taking One for the Team

Wiki and Leen took a more thorough accounting of Petey's workstation. It felt like they'd been in the egg-shaped room for hours, but it had barely been forty-five minutes according to the clock in Anna's office when they exited and returned to their quarters.

The trip back was much easier. A PeteyTech security guard escorted them personally, even allowing them to ride *inside* the elevator car. On the way back to the training hangar, Wiki got that strange, someone's-watching-me tingle at the back of her neck several times. Once when exiting the elevator in the PeteyTech Tower lobby. Again in the atrium. Again crossing the training floor on the way to their bunks. Each time she saw no discernible threat.

Leen noticed Wiki looking concerned. "Is something wrong?"

"You ever feel like you're being watched?"

"Sure. Especially when there are a lot of birds around. Some people believe birds are really government surveillance drones. I don't believe that. I think they're just nosy."

Wiki's unease was momentarily derailed by that birds-are-drones thing but quickly reset. Maybe she was just antsy and letting the throbbing headache from Petey's Egg get to her.

The only other soul they encountered was a custodian dusting off an informational plaque near one of the giant murals of astronauts on the moon—an elderly woman with her gray-black hair tied back with a scarf and her pushcart holding a blue plastic trash bin and miscellaneous cleaning supplies. She grinned the friendliest grin the girls had ever seen and waved eagerly as they passed her.

"Hi!" The girls waved back.

When they turned the corner for the camper quarters, their escort said, "Ignore Ally. She's sweet but a little . . ." He pointed at his temple and made a swirling motion. A mean gesture implying something was wrong with Ally the custodian, and Leen decided she'd put the escort at that top of her sabotage suspect list just because.

The lights in the sleeping quarters were dimmed since it was late, and it seemed all the other campers were in their cabins, asleep or otherwise occupied. Wiki pressed her camp ID to the sensor outside their door, disengaging the lock. Before their escort let them be, he said, "Mrs. Thunkle will expect daily reports on your progress. Instructions have been sent to your camp tablets."

Leen snapped off a sarcastic salute. "Sir! Yes, sir!"

Wiki said nothing. She sealed their cabin and changed into her pajamas, wrapped her hair, and tugged on her silk bonnet.

Leen changed too, then sat on the edge of her bunk, looking at Wiki, who lay flat on hers, her tablet grasped in a two-hand grip inches from her face.

Leen said, "I was thinking, we're going to have to balance two cases and whatever tasks camp requires. It'll be tough, but with both of us doing camp work, we can get through that twice as fast, then focus on—"

"No." Wiki didn't look up from her tablet.

"No like not twice as fast? Because by my calculation that math still holds."

"*No* we're not doing camp work together. Figured you'd be fine with that since I'm not supposed to be here."

Oh, Leen thought, *she's still angry about that.* "Wiki, I—"

"Didn't mean it?"

Leen's mouth opened, then shut.

Wiki said, "Thank you for not trying to lie about it. That would've made it worse."

Leen chose her next words carefully. "I'm sorry I said it."

"I believe that. It doesn't change a thing. Finding Petey and stopping the Interstellar-Z sabotage are Epic Ellisons cases. Cosmos Camp is not. Got it?"

Leen didn't get it. But Wiki placed her tablet in the cubby next to her bunk, then tugged her covers to her chin. "We can talk case stuff tomorrow night. Now I'm getting some rest. Busy day tomorrow."

"Okay," Leen said, a little bit angry but a little bit hurt too. "Good night."

Wiki grunted, then turned off the room lights from the smart panel near her bunk before Leen even had a chance to get settled. Though once she'd tucked herself in, sleep came fast for Leen. It seemed she'd simply blinked and it was day. She awoke to find Wiki gone, her bunk neatly made, like she'd never been there at all.

After showering, dressing, and making it to the cafeteria, Leen found her sister wrapping up breakfast with Kelvin, Sierra, and Britney. Something very funny must've happened because all of them were laughing too hard to finish their meals, handing their half-full trays to a sanitation bot making the rounds through the eatery. Leen grabbed some cereal and a muffin but found the only available seat was at a table with the unfriendly trio she'd met at the icebreaker. Harlow, Pierre, and Chest stared but didn't invite her over, and she didn't feel confident enough to invite herself. She flicked a glance toward Wiki's table, but they were already rising, en route to . . . somewhere. Maybe to tell each other more awesome jokes?

Wherever their destination, it was another place no one bothered to invite Leen.

Leen sat at their now-empty table and got two good spoonfuls of Frosty Loops down before Dr. Burr clapped her hands three times, the sound echoing. "Everyone in the training area. Three minutes!"

Two more spoonfuls, then Leen passed her tray to the Sani-Bot, telling herself this is fine. Everything's fine.

The hangar had been transformed since yesterday. The space where they'd had their virtual reality orientation, and got their first hint at Anna Thunkle's secret missions, was now divided into sections clearly marked by training equipment that Leen had seen in ThunkleTube videos. The 1/6th gravity chair. The whirling multi-axis trainer that simulated the effects of g-forces on the human body. The climbing wall built to look like a craft that you'd have to navigate in a space suit while on cables calibrated to make it feel like there was no gravity. Among other cool, cool things.

Despite the equipment crowding the space, there was still a lectern, but no chairs for the campers. Everyone stood. From this point on, even listening would be work.

Dr. Burr took to the lectern, dressed in a new Cosmos Camp jumpsuit—purple instead of the plain gray from yesterday.

"Okay, everyone," said Dr. Burr. "As you know, we'll have skills we practice on a daily basis along with team tasks over the next few weeks with the ultimate goal of your respective teams playing key roles in a Cosmos Camp simulated shuttle mission."

The campers cheered. Mostly. Leen cheered too, but it was pretend cheering. She knew that what she'd said about Wiki not belonging here was mean and, more importantly, wrong. Wiki may not invent things, but her brain was a computer brain. Nothing she put her mind to was beyond her grasp. It wasn't Wiki's fault Anna Thunkle pulled them both into a big old mess.

Dr. Burr said, "You may have noticed that I said respective teams . . . meaning that at some point I'll need to make a decision. PeteyTech has become the world's top technology company by encouraging competition. PeteyTech bests its competitors by thinking of innovative ideas first and bringing them to the marketplace before anyone else. The company's approach to space travel is no different. When the Interstellar Z launches—a historic event you campers will get to witness, yay—it will be the first craft to carry terraforming equipment to Mars."

Wait.

Wiki, who'd been smiling and enjoying her time with her new friends stiffened, her smile falling away. Mars? Leen had said the Interstellar-Z was going *to the moon*.

Maybe Wiki had gotten it wrong. Or maybe Dr. Burr had misspoken—though Wiki got the impression Dr. Burr never misspoke; she was magnificently precise.

Still, like so many other things that had been clashing with her not-so-reliable-lately memory, this troubled her in ways she didn't know how to express.

Dr. Burr went on. "When it comes time for the simulation, there will be a flight crew and there will be mission control—people on the ground. Both are equally important, but only one team will earn the responsibility of piloting a shuttle in our final simulated mission."

Low murmurs among the campers. Leen assumed everyone here wanted to be flight crew, not in mission control. You came here to get more cosmos than camp. At least that's how Leen felt about it.

She and Wiki would have to put their differences aside to win a coveted spot on the shuttle.

"With that in mind," Dr. Burr said, "choose your teams carefully based on your ultimate goal. I'll give you ten minutes to—"

Wiki raised her hand.

Dr. Burr said, "Yes?"

Wiki stood and swept her arm in the general direction of Sierra, Britney, and Kelvin. "We'd like to work together."

Leen's stomach fell.

"Are you sure?" Dr. Burr said, glancing at the remaining campers. "You have time to discuss. You may want to compare skills and specialties with your peers."

"We have, Dr. Burr, and we feel our skills go hand in hand." Wiki aimed a pointed look at Leen. "It's almost like we're *supposed* to be together."

Leen wilted while Dr. Burr nodded. "Very well, then. Your group will be Blue Team."

A training robot handed Wiki, Sierra, Britney, and Kelvin blue armbands to wear over their jumpsuits.

Dr. Burr directed her attention to Harlow, Pierre, and Chest, while Leen stood sort of off to the side by a commemorative space suit. "Any objections, Red Team?"

Harlow sneered at Leen. "A mild one but we'll make it work."

If Dr. Burr caught any of the venom in Harlow's voice, then she was comfortably immune. A training robot supplied their team with red armbands, then Dr. Burr clapped her hands—a sharp report—and said, "Shall we begin?"

And for the next two weeks, life at Cosmos Camps rocketed along like that. With Wiki and her team getting along splendidly, and Leen—thanks to the icy treatment from her unwelcoming team—getting exactly what she'd wished for: a unique experience all to herself.

It sucked.

COUNTDOWN
22:11:27:15

8

Cold Comfort (Just Kidding, It's Not Comfortable at All)

Petey Thunkle remained missing.

The girls were back in heavy parkas—provided by Pettygrew—along with earmuffs, knit caps, scarves, and mittens that peeled back at the fingertips so you could type. It was yet another evening in the arctic Egg that had them reexamining the same old physical clues from before (Petey's discarded clothing, his boring desk) and combing through gigabytes of data (while recognizing there were *terabytes* they couldn't touch because only Petey had the proper access). That night, though, Leen couldn't keep her mind on the task at hand. She kept zoning out and taking pictures of stuff she'd already photographed. The last two weeks of Cosmos Camp team competition had not gone . . . well, today being the worst yet.

Wiki, on the other hand, was energized from another great day with her great team accomplishing great things. She occupied Petey's chair as usual, digging into the pile of snacks she'd started bringing along on their nightly visits because all that greatness made you hungry and she thought better munching.

"I knew Sierra had killer reflexes," Wiki said through a mouthful of granola while marking folders and files she'd cleared as inconsequential to the investigation. "But who knew she'd be able to stabilize the multi-axis rig that fast? Best time in Cosmos Camp history! That's wild."

Leen retook scans of every surface of Petey's workstation, this time in the infrared light spectrum—a job handled mostly by the software in her goggles—giving her plenty of time to fret over how her own multi-axis performance had gone.

Sierra Ramos nabbed a record time while Leen had no record at all, since she never got the rig stabilized. She was locked in those concentric rings, spinning, spinning, spinning out of control for so long, Dr. Burr, with the most disappointed look Leen may have ever seen in her life, finally called it quits. Since the activity was meant to simulate the way a spacecraft can spin upon reentry into the Earth's atmosphere and stabilizing it meant saving the ship and everyone on board, let's just say Leen's nonperformance wasn't a great look for her team being picked to fly the shuttle simulation.

A point exasperated by Harlow loudly asking Dr. Burr if each team could drop its worst score. Or scorer.

Wiki groaned in Petey's chair. "I really wish they'd give us access to the supersecret stuff. I've got access to consumer products like the ThunklePhone and some info on the Interstellar-Z launch, but nothing more recent than that. Since the Egg and the Chicken are where he brainstormed new stuff, his disappearance is likely linked to whatever he was cooking up in here. But if I can't access his work, we're stuck. Have you found anything new?"

After lunch wasn't much better for Leen. They practiced putting on space suits, which required some help if you'd never gotten into one before. Wiki's team attacked the task like those superfast pit crews at the NASCAR races Daddy and Uncle Percy watched. In a series of blurs, everyone on Blue Team made it in and out of the suit with speed and precision. Harlow, Pierre, and Chest, on the other hand, sort of left Leen to her own devices when it was her turn to suit up and she ended up with her head stuck in the—

"Leen!" Wiki barked.

Leen snapped out of her funk, realizing she'd been scanning the same section of Petey's workstation, and the items laid upon it, for who knows how long.

"Are you okay?" Wiki asked, her eyebrow hooked up

like Mama's whenever she already knew the answer to the question.

"I'm fine. Nothing new to report."

Wiki spun Petey's chair toward Leen so they faced each other, a sleeve of Oreos in hand now and crumbs on her coat. "Let's go over it again. Petey locked himself in this room for more than a day. There are no cameras here and none outside the Egg, so we don't know if he left on his own or if something else happened. We have the clothes he left behind neatly folded on his chair, but I think it's safe to assume he wasn't sitting in here in his underwear. I hope."

"Yep!" Leen held up her mittens, her breaths coming out in white puffs. "He'd have turned into a block of ice."

"So he changed clothes. Why?" Wiki rubbed her temple and winced.

"What's wrong?"

"My head hurts. That's all. It's probably just the cold." Except . . . cold had never made Wiki's head hurt before. Yet whenever she stepped in this room, she felt like she needed aspirin and a nap.

She munched more cookies, then reached for her carton of milk to wash them down. She'd brought the milk in the night before but hadn't opened it. Thank goodness it was as cold as a refrigerator in the Egg because she'd have to throw it away otherwise.

Still, even if this cold wasn't making her head hurt, the frigid temperature sure made it hard to think.

Wiki said, "Why would Petey build a room like this and keep it this cold if this is where he'd brainstorm new innovations? How could he stay here for a day at a time, even if he was in the warmest clothes around?"

So many questions that all had to have answers, yet Wiki's thumping headache was getting in the way of her reasoning, and Leen was just not all there. Wiki opened her milk, raised the carton toward her lips, then winced away fighting a gag.

The milk smelled terrible. It had gone bad. "Ewww."

Leen waved a hand in front of her nose, smelling it too. "Wow! How old is that?"

"Not very."

The expiration date was still a week away. But most likely the milk had spoiled before she'd even brought it into the Egg, or it had been mishandled when it was delivered to the Cosmos Camp cafeteria. Wiki resealed the carton. What a waste. "Maybe we should call it a night. See if some sleep helps."

She meant help her headache as much as their understanding of this strange, strange case.

"Sure." Leen deactivated her goggles and raised them to her forehead. "Whatever."

Wiki spun toward the computer bank, intending to shut

it down, but the Interstellar-Z folder she'd opened now had a flashing message over it.

Syncing . . .

"Hey, Leen. Look at this."

Leen scuttled over, her head tilting. "Expand it so I can see the subfolders."

Wiki did just that, opening a window that listed hundreds—if not thousands—of subfolders, but the one being altered was flashing right at the top: *Navigation Calculations.*

Leen reached across Wiki and clicked. The folder opened a complicated list of mathematical equations that were changing right before their eyes.

"The saboteur," they said together.

"Can you tell where this is coming from?" Wiki asked.

Leen nudged Wiki's chair out of the way before she finished the question. "On it."

Through a series of quick keystrokes, Leen accessed some hidden menus. A few more commands, and she was able to get an approximate location for the terminal these changes were being made from, but given how her day had gone, she immediately wondered if she'd messed up somehow.

"Well?" Wiki said.

Leen, uncertain but forging ahead anyway, said, "It's coming from Cosmos Camp."

Like Spaghetti but Reversed

The changes were being keyed into a computer terminal in the Cosmos Camp training hangar. Specifically, the terminal in Dr. Burr's office. A quick check of the security logs by Wiki confirmed Dr. Burr went home two hours ago.

Since, to Wiki and Leen's knowledge, they were the only ones who sorta kinda had permission to be out of their bunks after hours, it stood to reason that the person currently making changes to the Interstellar-Z launch data was up to no good and this could be a break in at least one of the mysteries Anna Thunkle had tasked them with solving to save their family's farm.

Leen reasoned if she could scratch "catch the saboteur" off her to-do list, it'd free up more brain power for sulking over how badly her time on Red Team was going.

The girls snuck back down to the hangar. This time of night, in the dimmed lighting, the hangar was crowded with not only training equipment and museum exhibits, but also shadows and spooky sounds. Which was awesome but in a sarcastic way, which meant it wasn't awesome in the slightest.

They crept around the training equipment that had perplexed Leen so much earlier. Monitors in the mini flight simulators glowed blue, casting flickering specters all the way to the ceiling. Recordings of historical shuttle launches and capsule reentries played on wall-mounted TVs in a low-volume loop, as if astronauts were whispering to them from the past. Beyond the training floor were museum displays of moon rocks and space junk and space shuttle food, and space shuttle junk food (nothing about a freeze-dried cheeseburger sounded fun). Past all that, the office where nobody should be.

Dr. Burr's office had big glass windows blocked by blinds. During the day the blinds were parted so you could see inside, though the doctor was mostly on the floor guiding them through camp activities. Now the blinds were closed, though a desk lamp silhouetted a trespasser hunched over Dr. Burr's computer.

The girls took cover behind a satellite exhibit, plotting.

"We don't actually have to catch them," Wiki said, removing her ThunklePhone from her hip pocket. "A picture should do it."

Leen nodded. "Not like we have anything to tie them up with or shock them into submission. I wish I'd brought one of my drones."

Wiki's face tightened, displeased. "I thought the Department of Defense made you turn over all your drones."

Leen quickly changed the subject. "On three . . ." She counted it off with her fingers. One . . . two . . .

They rushed Dr. Burr's door. Leen flung it open, while Wiki leapt into position to get the best shot of the intruder. This close, by the light of Burr's desk lamp, Wiki understood the mistake she'd made peering through the training hangar gloom.

The blinds weren't closed or even lowered. They were locked in place at the top of the window frame, giving a full, unobstructed view of the hangar exhibits from this side of the glass. From the other side of the glass, they'd had a clear view into the office. They'd never been looking at the saboteur's *shadow*.

The saboteur *was* a shadow.

Or as inky dark as one.

Wiki's camera flashed! But the thing was eel-quick, slinging it's lanky, fluid body out of the lens's view. It moved like a liquid and a solid, ricocheting off the wall with a sound like wet slaps, before angling for a ventilation grate in the ceiling.

The girls watched, bug-eyed, as the being divided itself

and squeezed through the vent slits in strands, something like Mama's pasta maker running in reverse.

Within a few seconds, its whole body had entered the overhead vents with a final *slurp*. The girls didn't waste time voicing their awe-horror-disbelief—though they felt plenty. Instead, they ran from the office, following the bulging aluminum shaft overhead in an attempt to track that whatever the heck.

It thumped and bucked along while the girls zigzagged around exhibits at a full sprint, trying to keep pace. A futile effort.

The shaft angled up, then through the perimeter wall, allowing that thing to escape to who knew where! Wiki and Leen could only stare at that last section of shaft. Out of breath. Panting.

"Did you," Leen said, gasping, "at least get a photo?"

Wiki checked the pics on her phone. All she had was a shot of Dr. Burr's computer and a tiny tendril of the shadow saboteur escaping.

"We blew it," Wiki said.

"It could be worse, I guess."

An alarm blared. Red emergency lights flashed in every corner. A mechanical voice shouted through the speaker system. "Alert! Alert! Intruders in the training hangar. Alert!"

Within seconds PeteyTech security, the Cosmos Camp

training bots, and all their fellow campers appeared, some rubbing sleep from their eyes and cinching robes over their pajamas.

The guards shined flashlights directly on the darkly clothed Ellisons. Wiki slapped a palm to her forehead, while Leen waved at everyone. "Hi!"

10

Epic Expectations

The next morning Wiki and Leen sat outside Anna Thunkle's office listening to Dr. Burr's muffled yells through the doors.

The vacuuming robot assistant that was Pettygrew zoomed to the girls, projecting the AI hologram whose sympathetic face did little to comfort them, despite her words.

"It's not as bad as it sounds," said Pettygrew.

"Really?" said Wiki. "Because even if it's half as bad as it sounds, it's still pretty bad."

Pettygrew's eyes cut left, as if she was looking through Anna's office door. Dr. Burr had stopped yelling, so the girls heard nothing.

Pettygrew said, "Anna has succeeded in calming down Dr. Burr and is now explaining why it was necessary to employ your particular set of skills in some delicate company matters."

"How do you know that?" asked Leen.

"Because I am patched into the ThunkleBand Communications System that runs throughout the facility."

"You're eavesdropping!" the girls said together.

"Wouldn't you if you could?"

The AI had a point. The only reason they weren't soaking up every bit of the conversation being had about them and their futures at Cosmos Camp was because the walls here were too thick to allow it.

More thumping sounds—Dr. Burr's yelling—from inside the office.

"What are they saying now?" Leen asked.

"You're about to see. Good luck. Bye!" The hologram winked from view and the vacuum zipped around the corner as if running for its life.

Awesome.

The doors swung open as if Dr. Burr kicked them. Her head whipped toward the girls. "Come. Now."

The doctor marched to the elevator, and the girls did not linger. They caught up just as the doors opened, with only Leen sparing a glance into the office where Anna rubbed her belly as if Baby Thunkle needed a soothing massage.

I'd like a soothing massage, Leen thought as Wiki tugged her into the elevator car.

For at least five floors, Dr. Burr said nothing. Wiki, who always preferred her bad news straight because she wanted her unpleasant forever memories neat and easy to bury under every other forever memory, asked, "Are you kicking us out of Cosmos Camp?"

Dr. Burr exhaled, the breath whistling past her lips. "If it were up to me, I'd have you both sent home by end of day. That is not within my power, though."

That should be good news. They were staying. Yet hearing the only adult here who looked like them wish she could send them home stung. Wiki and Leen deflated, but Leen especially. This woman was her idol, and it seemed like she kind of hated the Ellison sisters.

Dr. Burr said, "Oh, don't look at me like I'm about to eat you whole. It's not because I dislike you. It's because I want to protect you from whatever shenanigans the Thunkles are up to. Why should you two bear the burden of 'investigating' their mess-ups? You're kids!"

Wiki said, "Dr. Burr, we've been doing this sort of thing for a long time."

"Back home. For your community. I'm sure the people of Slogan Province—"

"Logan County," Leen corrected.

"Yes, that place. I'm sure they're grateful. That's not what you're here to do. Do any of the other children here have to be part-time detectives while enduring the rigors of the Cosmos Camp training program? *We* are always the ones expected to do double duty and be happy about it. For exposure. Or for the greater good. Or for some reward that's never quite what's promised. Then it's still not enough. *We're* expected to show gratitude for being obligated to a single, limited role for all of our best years. *We* prepare the company for its future, but the company doesn't prepare us for ours."

Wiki squinted and scrutinized—the doctor's tone, her facial tics, the body language. That's when Wiki knew: Dr. Burr wasn't at PeteyTech, or Cosmos Camp, because she *wanted* to be here.

"What did you have to do for them?" Wiki asked.

Dr. Burr got quiet as the elevator dinged and opened at the lobby. "A story for another time, dears. For now, get in that hangar with your teams. You've got some catching up to do."

Wiki and Leen parted ways somewhat surprised that they were still, officially, Cosmos Campers. They headed to opposite ends of the training hangar to rejoin their teams. Wiki's team practiced reading a shuttle's instrument panel with their training robot, Sam, while Leen's team manipulated a mechanical arm to make shuttle hull repairs with their robot trainer, Ralph.

Leen hovered at the back of the group, as she'd been used to doing since they didn't actually talk to her, hoping to learn by observation. She watched Chest work two large handles in a huge panel like a giant video-game controller. He maneuvered the left stick and the arm tracked up and down. Adjustments to the right stick moved the arm side to side or front to back. The team and the control panel were separated from the arm and the section of shuttle it was repairing by a thick pane of glass.

From yesterday's training, Leen knew that every exercise began with a scenario, some imaginary situation to help them wrap their heads around how all sorts of unexpected things can happen in space and how you have to be prepared for all of it because it's not like getting a flat tire on the side of the road. You can't call a tow truck for help; you have to be able to take your spare out of the trunk and put it on yourself. In space. So to speak.

Leen's observations were interrupted when Harlow thrust her Whistleberry in front of Leen's face. On its display, Leen found herself looking at . . . herself. And Wiki. An old picture from the *Logan County Gazette* with the headline EPIC ELLISONS RECEIVE THIRD KEY TO THE CITY.

"Epic Ellisons." Harlow got nose to nose with Leen. "Explain."

Ghosts, Aliens, and Probabilities, Oh My!

Wiki's team gave her a lot of side-eye when she returned to the group, and there'd surely be questions at their next break, but Kelvin, Sierra, and Britney took their training very seriously and did not lose focus on Sam's instrument instructions for very long. Wiki, on the other hand, was still struck by Dr. Burr's words and the meaning behind them.

We *are always the ones expected to do double duty and be happy about it.*

Wiki knew by "we" the doctor meant Black girls and women. Mama often told them something similar—usually with Daddy nodding and rubbing her back and asking her if there was any more he could do to help.

Mama and Dr. Burr's point was not lost. Petey Thunkle got himself into a mess, and Anna Thunkle summoned Wiki and her sister to clean it up. Sure, there would be rewards if they pulled it off, but it all was starting to feel wrong somehow. Way wrong.

Also, there was the little matter of the shape-shifting shadow creature altering calculations for the Interstellar-Z launch. Which was concerning.

Though Wiki wanted to know where Petey Thunkle was and what sort of mischief that murky creature was trying to cause, she didn't like feeling taken advantage of.

Mama once said, "You need to set boundaries, the way everyone else does, to take care of yourself. You also need to be ready when folks treat you different for it. People show you how they really feel when you *don't* do what they want."

Sam finished his explanation of the instrument panel and each team member took turns playing "commander," adjusting the stick through simulated landings. If they got off course or toggled an incorrect switch, the screen would tint red and flash a warning until they corrected their mistake. Wiki went last, and though she picked up enough from observing others to complete a near-perfect touchdown, she took opportunities to make incorrect decisions to test the warning software. When she finished, something occurred to her.

"Sam, we're practicing landings. But how much of the rest does a commander handle?"

"Very little," Sam said robotically.

"So computer calculations are responsible for most of the takeoff and flight?"

"Correct. That is the best way to get the shuttle to where it's going safely."

"What if something changed the calculations at the last minute? Couldn't the astronauts be in danger of a disaster?"

"Yes and no. They could be in danger, but we have thorough safety systems. Any alterations that would endanger the crew would result in an aborted launch."

That was good to know. Yet it did make Wiki question how good the safety systems were. Anything smart enough to alter the shuttle's navigation programming the way that sabotaging creature seemed to be would know the safety system was going to flag their changes, right? Unless . . .

"Sam, is there any way the safety systems wouldn't catch changes to the flight computer's calculations?"

"Yes," Sam said, "if the changes were safe."

A bunch more questions exploded in Wiki's brain like corn kernels popping. She stopped herself from asking them all because Kelvin, Britney, and Sierra were staring at her bug-eyed. She backed down for the moment and realized, though she would indeed set boundaries and take care of herself, it probably wouldn't be today.

Because now she wondered if, maybe, the shadow

91

creature—despite being a shadow creature—*wasn't* actually sabotaging the launch.

If that was the case, was Anna Thunkle confused about the whole thing or . . .

Had she lied to them?

At lunch, for the first time, Red Team's attention was entirely on Leen . . . captivated.

She finished up another story: ". . . and it turned out the farmer's market thieves were hiding the money they stole from other sellers inside fake loaves of bread."

Chest leaned forward. "You figured that out with an insectile drone of your own design?"

"Drone sounds so impersonal. I like to call him Dewey. And Wiki helped too."

"You did build the device—I mean, Dewey—though?" Pierre asked.

"Sure. I build stuff all the time."

Harlow's arms were crossed, her face expressionless. Leen braced herself for something mean.

"Unimpressed," Harlow said before breaking into a wide smile.

Leen kept her face still, though she quaked inside. "Well, I don't know what to tell you. That's my life, and it's exciting whether you agree or not."

"Not," Harlow chirped. "However, I was always told it's better to show than tell."

"What's that mean?"

"Have you seen this afternoon's activity? If you're as epic as you say you are . . . win us the day."

Leen grabbed her camp tablet and opened the training app. For the first time since arrival week, she perked up.

Today's Concept: Rocket Design.

Leen grinned. "Challenge accepted."

Kelvin, Sierra, and Britney did their best not to pry or ask questions that might not be their business, but Wiki read their tics, and even someone without an eidetic memory and encyclopedic knowledge of human behavior would've noticed the totally unsubtle way they avoided looking at her. Wiki dropped her fork, and it clinked loudly on her tray of half-eaten food. Enough. "Me and my sister solve mysteries, fight weird stuff, and are generally epic. I am willing to take any questions you may have about the three topics mentioned."

Britney let out a relieved breath. "Thank goodness. I want to know all of the things!"

And so began a barrage that had Wiki recounting adventures in Logan County and much of what the campers had walked in on the night before, without mentioning *why* they were investigating things at PeteyTech. It was not her place to reveal that Petey Thunkle was missing.

Still, what she did reveal—a shape-shifting creature messing with computer systems—is pretty much where their focus remained.

Sierra said, "Given what you've described of the creature, it must be supernatural or extraterrestrial. Would you agree?"

"A ghost or an alien?" Kelvin hemmed a little, hawed a bit. "I don't know. There's not a ton to go on. Wiki, you and your sister only saw it for a moment, right?"

Wiki nodded. That was true. Though Kelvin's tics screamed *skepticism* or perhaps *worry*. He'd been dedicated to making sure their team was the one in the cockpit for the final simulation, and too much attention on Wiki and Leen's sideshow might throw them off track. It seemed, most likely, that would be the root of his concern.

Britney said, "Humans can't 'flow into vents,' so Sierra's assumption is at least a good working hypothesis. Until we know more."

Usually these discussions would be strictly between her and Leen, but it was nice to bounce ideas off a few new minds who might see something they had missed.

Wiki said, "Since PeteyTech and Cosmos Camp are focused on science, I'd be willing to exclude supernatural entities for the time being."

Kelvin scoffed. "You think there's an *alien* here at Cosmos Camp?"

"It's possible," Wiki said. But was it *probable*?

The training robots bopped to the center of the cafeteria in their uncanny strides that seemed quick but also like they were moving through syrup. They spoke in unison. "Please report to the training hangar for this afternoon's workshop."

Across the way, Leen's team was way more animated than usual. And smiling. Strange.

There was an extra creepy expression on that Harlow girl, kind of like if a wolf smiled at you. She looped an arm over Leen's shoulder, and they left the cafeteria in rapid-fire conversation. Almost friendly. That, too, was strange.

Hmm.

The training hangar had undergone a conversion once again. Now there were two long tables—one for each team—and slim touch-screen computers with virtual reality headsets and fancy gloves that looked like they'd fit a hockey goalie. Dr. Burr stood between the tables and addressed the campers.

"Welcome to the rocket design challenge!" She motioned to the workstations. "You'll consult with your team to design a rocket on paper first, then you'll don your VR headsets and gloves to build a 3D model of your team's design inside the Cosmos Camp system. Designs will be judged on innovation, efficiency, and aerodynamics. While the team with the best design will be awarded points toward their role in the final simulation, please do have fun and be creative. Every innovation in human history was something that seemed impossible at one time. You have two hours!"

The teams rushed to their respective stations, and while Wiki's team engaged in rapid chatter, Harlow hushed Chest and Pierre immediately. Her eyes on Leen, she said, "Well?"

Leen smirked. "I thought you'd never ask."

12

All That from Corn?

Two hours later, when Dr. Burr had the teams finalize their designs in the system for her review, she began with Wiki's team.

"Nice. Very traditional. I see what you did with the nose cones on the shuttle and the individual boosters. You may need to move the lattice fins higher to properly compensate for drag, giving you better control, but even at a glance, this is a sound design." She went on, praising changes she agreed with and pointing out to the entire group additional considerations whenever you make such a change. She finished with "Never be afraid to think boldly and challenge what supposedly can't be done. Now, the next design."

Dr. Burr swiped across her screen, bringing Leen's design up.

Her head tilted.

Her lips pursed.

She looked to the team, clearly confused. "What is this?"

Harlow, the official spokesperson for the team, said, "*Our* rocket."

"Young lady"—Dr. Burr looked at the monitor, then at Harlow, then back at the monitor—"I can see that. But why is it *yellow*?"

The rocket displayed looked quite conventional, almost an exact replica of the Interstellar-Z rocket outside the hangar windows, except for the color. Everyone awaited Red Team's explanation.

Leen cleared her throat. "Did you know about all the various uses for peanuts that Black inventor George Washington Carver came up with? A lot! He figured out over three hundred ways to use peanuts that most people wouldn't think to use peanuts for. There's the food stuff, which is, duh, obvious. Then there was stuff like soap and cleaning products and even wood stain—"

"Ms. Ellison," Dr. Burr interrupted, "I know who George Washington Carver is. I know all about the peanuts. What's that got to do with this?"

"Um, I was always inspired by how many things you can do with a peanut. Me and my family don't grow peanuts, though. We grow corn. So I did a bunch of stuff with corn."

Wiki leaned forward, getting a hint of what was happening here.

Keep going, Wiki thought. *You got this.*

Leen stopped talking like she sometimes did when stuff made sense to her but she sensed it maybe didn't make sense to anyone else. Wiki had seen this many times and, despite the mild bickering they'd been up to lately, willed her sister to snap out of it because she'd also seen the look on Leen's face when she'd concocted something brilliant. That look was on Leen's face right now.

Dr. Burr asked, "Is this some sort of corn-based stain then?"

"Yes," said Leen.

"How is this an innovation?"

"Because it's more of an organogel than a stain. A complex coating that not only absorbs heat but reduces friction to almost nothing. My theory is if you coat a rocket in that, there'd be way less air resistance at takeoff. Less resistance would allow the vehicle to burn less fuel when leaving the atmosphere. Less fuel means less weight, less pollution, less cost."

Dr. Burr's jaw looked loose. "You're serious? From corn?"

Leen hesitated. Was Dr. Burr upset? "Yep."

"It's yellow because it's made of corn?"

Leen's insides quivered. Her voice got small. Had she somehow messed up again? All her calculations were sound. She'd triple-checked. "I suppose I could change the color, but since it is from corn, I figure corn should get the credit."

Dr. Burr touched the display with her thumb and fore-finger, swiping and pinching at the screen in a way that rotated Red Team's rocket design in various angles.

The doctor took a deep breath and let out a heavy sigh.

Wiki's stomach became a pit. What was Dr. Burr about to say to Leen?

If it were up to me, I'd have you both sent home by end of day.

"This is well beyond the scope of the assignment, Ms. Ellison," Dr. Burr began.

Harlow and the rest of their team radiated malice in the moment. If an ominous storm cloud could be people, it would be them.

"I ordered your team to design a rocket. I expected something that showed ingenuity but was also feasible for a present-day launch. What you did—"

Leen's shoulders slumped, and her eyes dropped to the floor, anticipating her dragging.

"—was so far beyond my wildest expectations that I may just revamp this entire exercise for future Cosmos Campers." Dr. Burr cast her eyes upward, as if reading a sign only she could see. "Design a rocket using ecofriendly materials from your region!"

Leen went bug-eyed. "You like it?"

"Ms. Ellison, it's fantastic. Congratulations to you and your team. You all are the winners of today's contest."

Harlow, Pierre, and Chest rushed Leen, wrapping her up in a congratulatory group hug. And Wiki, happier than maybe the moment justified since their win meant her team's loss, forgot about all that competition stuff and cheered for her sister too. Sierra, Britney, and Kelvin offered polite, deserved applause, but their faces projected another message: *if the goal was to be the shuttle crew on final simulation day, then we might be in trouble.*

Dr. Burr said, "Now I'm really looking forward to our tour of the Interstellar-Z launch facility tomorrow. Teams, be ready to discuss your ideas with the engineers over there. Okay?"

Leen and her team gushed. What an opportunity!

Too bad it wouldn't last.

No sneaking that night! The girls settled into their bunks early. Leen kept reviewing and tweaking her rocket design in preparation for tomorrow's Interstellar-Z tour, while Wiki reviewed the hundreds and hundreds of photos they'd taken of Petey Thunkle's Chicken and Egg, hoping something new would leap out at her. It was mind-numbing work swiping through the images. Her eyes tired, and every so often she blinked rapidly to stay awake. In the midst of one of those blinks, her eyes just didn't open.

She recognized briefly that she was dozing off, the tablet resting on her chest as it rose slower and slower, peaceful slumber overtaking her, followed by dreaming.

No one knew this, but Wiki enjoyed dreaming more than

any other mental exercise. She remembered everything she saw and heard when awake, so dreams offered her an experience most people seemed to take for granted: forgetting.

Dreams were hard to remember, no matter how much Wiki tried. Based on the occasional question she posed, and her own research, that seemed common and thus exciting because it meant, for once, her brain did something like everyone else's. There was an exception, though. Quite an unpleasant one.

Nightmares.

For the better part of the last year, they'd come unexpectedly. And tonight's was a doozy! She was back in Logan County, and school was still in session. As bad as that was, it wasn't the nightmarish part.

Mr. Rickard, the science teacher, scribbled notes on the board about Thomas Edison, Nikola Tesla, and George Westinghouse—three men who played a direct role in how we use electricity today. Mr. Rickard said, "These men of science battled to prove each had superior ideas for utilizing electrical current. It was a whole thing. Then—"

Mr. Rickard stood very still, reevaluating his notes. He grabbed the eraser and said, "Sorry, class, I was wrong. Dr. Frankenstein is the inventor of electricity."

This was all very hazy in that way dreams can sometimes be, but even through the gauzy soft focus of nighttime imaginings, Wiki was certain Dr. Frankenstein didn't invent electricity since Dr. Frankenstein was a fictional character.

Mr. Rickard seemed convinced, and he dragged the eraser across his previous notes in a wide arc. The motion should've left behind a section of bare whiteboard. Instead, the eraser left a trail of darkness. Full, all-encompassing darkness.

He kept erasing the notes on Edison, Tesla, and Westinghouse. With each pass of the eraser, more of reality was swept away until the whiteboard was a rectangular portal to an abyss.

Mr. Rickard faced the class then, paying particular attention to his desk. "The inventor of desks is Dr. Jekyll."

Wiki didn't know who the inventor of desks was; she only knew it wasn't Dr. Jekyll, since he was also a fictional character. It became a trivial point when Mr. Rickard touched his desk with his eraser and the heavy piece of furniture was sucked into the void behind him.

Bryan Donovan sat in the front row—just four seats ahead of Wiki—studiously taking notes when Mr. Rickard approached and said, "Dr. Emmett Brown invented you."

He touched Bryan with the eraser. The boy, and his desk, flipped end over end into the abyss. Bryan still appeared to be taking notes when the darkness consumed him.

Mr. Rickard continued to the next student, pronouncing some other fictional scientist *invented them*, before banishing them to the sucking portal at the front of the room. Leen occupied the seat in front of Wiki's, dutifully taking notes like everyone else, oblivious to the terrible happenings.

"Leen! Leen!" Wiki tried to free herself from her own seat, tried to protect her sister as Mr. Rickard hovered over her.

He wasn't Mr. Rickard anymore, though.

He was Petey Thunkle.

Petey told Leen, "*I* invented *you*."

He reached for her with the eraser, and—

"Wiki! Wiki, wake up!"

Wiki wrestled herself from the nightmare's claws and into the protective arms of her sister. A groggy Leen, half-asleep herself but operating on comforting autopilot, rocked Wiki and whispered, "You're fine. Just a bad dream."

It was. It was. Yet whenever it happened and it was that bad, it felt like so much more.

It embarrassed Wiki that she had so little control over how she reacted—in both the dreaming and real worlds—during the nightmares. "I'm sorry for waking you up. I know you have a big day tomorrow."

Leen yawned and returned to her own bunk. "Big day for all of us. Seeing the Interstellar-Z anti-friction coating up close will be cool, I guess. I don't know how PeteyTech thinks of this stuff."

Wiki lay there, staring at the ceiling, waiting for Leen's soft snoring before she got out of bed and snuck from their bunk. Because she'd heard her sister clearly, and the phrase "Interstellar-Z anti-friction coating" made her wonder if maybe she hadn't woken from her nightmare at all.

Leen could be mixed-up, Wiki reasoned. She was half-asleep and had maybe mashed up the details of the anti-friction coating she'd invented with the expectation of visiting the shuttle later that day.

Wiki would just tiptoe to the back of the training hangar to be sure.

She slipped from their quarters and wasted no time getting to the training floor. She weaved around equipment and exhibits, past Dr. Burr's office (which was thankfully empty), and all the way to the far wall, where she had to climb on some crates to peer through the high windows for a glimpse of the rocket in the distance.

The entire time she approached the glass, she'd been telling herself she'd see the same old shuttle she'd been glimpsing in the distance for the last couple of weeks. At the same time, she'd hoped and prayed and wished she wouldn't see what she was afraid of.

At the window, she gained an unobstructed view of the launchpad. Her harsh gasp fogged the glass, and she wiped the condensation away with the heel of her hand.

No.

How?

The spacecraft seated on the launchpad wasn't the patriotic red, white, and blue she'd seen yesterday, and every day, since she'd arrived at Cosmos Camp. The Interstellar-Z was now a bright neon yellow.

Wiki corrected herself.

Not *neon* yellow.

Corn yellow.

Nightmare Petey Thunkle sounded off in Wiki's head: *I invented you.*

She wanted to say that he was wrong—as wrong as Dr. Frankenstein inventing electricity—but she honestly didn't know what to think anymore.

13

Where the People Aren't

Wiki hadn't said much since Leen woke up . . . other than to rub in how bad things had gone yesterday.

Red Team's "conventional and uninspired" rocket design hadn't impressed Dr. Burr. At. All.

The whole time Leen had worked on it, Harlow had been like, "I thought you built stuff epically, or whatever, where you come from."

Leen had tried defending herself because, yes, she designed and built stuff all the time back home. Here, she couldn't seem to get out of her own way. She'd wanted to make some improvements on traditional rocket designs but had had trouble thinking of concepts better than what Petey-Tech had already done with Interstellar-Z's genius coating. Blue Team had won the design competition, so Wiki must've been in a meanie mood to ask the stuff she was asking.

"Leen, how long have you known about the Interstellar-Z being yellow?"

"Leen, you don't remember PeteyTech designing a rocket that was red, white, and blue like the American flag?"

"Leen, what other PeteyTech stuff have you always known about?"

Leen supposed those were jokes at her expense or something. She didn't exactly get them. Maybe they were some Blue Team insider gags? She got the point, though. The thing Leen had said about Wiki not belonging here wasn't so accurate. If she needed to spot an Ellison sister who didn't belong at Cosmos Camp, the mirror was on the back of their bunk door.

Their Interstellar-Z tour was the first thing on the day's schedule and would last all the way until lunch. Dr. Burr, Sam, and Ralph led the campers over in a big, chatty group . . . that Leen trailed, saying nothing.

Probably for the best.

Dr. Burr stopped them at the entrance of the launch center. "As you can see, this is the third of four massive structures on the PeteyTech campus: our home at the Cosmos Camp training hangar, the corporate tower, here, at Interstellar-Z Mission Control, and"—she motioned toward the unobstructed view of the massive rocket positioned between Mission Control and the ocean— "that beauty of a ship you'll see launch before you return home."

The doctor ushered the class deeper into the facility, but Wiki stared at the launch clock. Leen remained salty over Wiki's weird, prickly questions, but she didn't want her sister to get left behind.

"Hey," Leen said, "we're moving."

Wiki shook her head and scurried along. "Right. Tour."

Leen stared after her sister. What was up with Wiki today?

They got to see Interstellar-Z Mission Control: a series of computer terminals positioned in front of a huge monitor the size of a movie-theater screen; the wind tunnels for testing engine designs; then the break room for getting delicious snacks and beverages (Harlow insisted on making a mocha caramel latte, which was annoying, but everyone's feet hurt from walking all over the place so whatever). Finally . . .

"To the ship!" said Dr. Burr.

It was a slog out to the launchpad, a mile at least. There were golf carts parked outside of the mission control facility, yet it occurred to Leen that not only could the campers (probably) not drive the carts but there didn't seem to be anyone around who could.

They'd seen the reception area, computer stations, even a place to make delicious coffee (if Leen didn't find coffee disgusting). But where were the people?

The closer they got to the towering Interstellar-Z and those working the scaffolding surrounding it, Leen understood. You didn't need a lot of people when you had a lot of robots.

Training robots Sam and Ralph greeted another robot who wore a hard hat and seemed to have a fabricated and unnecessary belly. He made a motion as if he were tugging up his pants, though he had no pants. It reminded Leen of a farmhand who worked for Daddy with a similar gut who always had to pull up his pants so no one saw his butt crack . . . he was rarely successful.

The big-bellied robot spoke in a jerky, digitized voice, "Hello, campers, I'm Fred the Foreman."

"Hi, Fred!" everyone but Harlow said. She was finishing her latte.

Fred took over the tour by issuing all the campers hard hats and walking them through the safe areas around the launchpad. Moving along the scaffolding and rappelling down the sides of the ship on cables with welding torches for hands were more robots. Some wore coveralls. Some wore jeans and plaid shirts and work boots.

Fred led the campers as close as they could get to the base of the ship, explaining the wisdom of the yellow coating, which was an echo of Leen's explanation from the previous day—or so Wiki, and only Wiki, recalled.

Wiki raised her hand, grabbing Fred's attention.

Fred said, "Yes, young carbon-based life-form?"

"How did PeteyTech get the idea for the coating?"

"Oh, it's a special blend created by Petey Thunkle for the express purposes of this mission. It will allow the boosters to use—"

"Less fuel. Yes, got that."

The image on Fred's tablet face switched from a talking emoji to a wide-mouthed surprise emoji, then back to talking. "You know your aerodynamics well."

Not me, Wiki thought. *Leen.*

Then she asked her question again. "But how did the company get the idea?"

Fred's emoji face tilted as if the answer was obvious. "Petey Thunkle is the greatest innovator of this time."

Wiki's face screwed up like she was working some tough calculation. Leen noticed.

Dr. Burr blinked rapidly, her tics showing concern. "Okay, then. Fred, if you're ready to wrap up, we'll conclude today's tour and get you campers fed."

Upbeat murmurs from the hungry group confirmed that lunch was indeed desired. While Leen's appetite was insistent, her suspicions over Wiki being up to something took a much bigger bite of her attention.

⚡ ⚡ ⚡

The Blue and Red Teams took different tables at lunch, and Wiki noticed that even though the Red Team shared a table, they put several seats between them and Leen, who mostly stared at her tray. The memory of Leen being her team's hero only a day ago clashed with this more consistent role of Leen being an outsider on the Red Team. If Leen didn't really design the corn-based organogel coating to win the competition, then there were no new reasons for Harlow, Pierre, and Chest to treat her better.

How did that happen, though?

Wiki was frustrated by the sheer impossibility of it all but was over the idea that something was wrong with *her*. Oh no. Something was wrong with *PeteyTech*. Very wrong.

That she was sure of.

This was a puzzle, making it harder to figure out. Harder but not impossible. Wiki's brain worked on assembling the pieces she had into the big picture, ignoring the food before her completely.

Until Britney grabbed a milk carton.

Through the haze of deduction, of nudging each clue against the other to see if they fit, Wiki recognized the milk as the same she'd had to toss the last time she and Leen had been in the Egg. The carton had the same dairy farm emblem and the same expiration date. Wiki's internal alarm sounded when Britney opened it and brought the carton to her lips.

"Don't," Wiki said. "It's a bad batch."

Britney was already gulping, her eyes widening. She lowered the carton quick, examining it. "What's wrong?"

"It's just—" Wiki stopped talking. If the milk were bad, Britney wouldn't have had to hear it from her. She'd have smelled it, tasted it, on her own. "I'm sorry. I had a carton of the same milk and it was completely spoiled."

"Wow. That sucks. This is from the best dairy farm around. I know because back home my cousins live on a dairy farm and they got excited when they heard I was coming here. This milk is naturally sweet. You should try some of mine if yours was bad."

Britney offered, but Wiki declined from the memory alone. "I can still smell mine. No thanks."

"Maybe yours didn't make it into a fridge in time?"

"No." Given the temp in the Egg, refrigeration shouldn't have been an issue. "It was plenty cold."

Britney shrugged. "That's just weird. If it was refrigerated, it should've taken days to spoil. Who knows?"

That's when the puzzle pieces slammed into place. Most of them, if not *all* of them! Wiki . . . *knew*. As strong of a hunch as she'd ever had.

She popped up from the table, nearly sprinting, though she heard Britney say, "If you're going to grab another milk—because I can see you're excited—bring me one!"

Wiki wasn't grabbing milk. She grabbed Leen.

"Hey! I think I know where Petey is. Or maybe *when* he is. Or maybe—well, I'm not one hundred percent sure about the details, but we need to hit the Egg. Tonight!"

Wiki was so excited, and loud, it never occurred to her that even though Harlow, Pierre, and Chest barely tolerated the sight of Leen, it did not mean they weren't listening.

14
Eggs, Lightning Side Up

Concentrating on the afternoon's regularly scheduled camp activities, then suffering through dinner, then calmly "turning in for the night" was a struggle. Wiki worked over the conclusions she'd come to. There were plenty of holes to poke in her deductions, that much was true. The more she turned them over in her mind, the more confident she felt she was angling in the right direction. No matter how weird that direction was.

Leen did not share Wiki's confidence. She didn't have a lot of her own confidence anymore either. Cosmos Camp was nothing like what she'd dreamed. She'd thought she'd find her purpose here, a true calling. Instead, it was a bunch of humiliating failures, one after another. Maybe that was her calling: failed tinkerer building things no one wanted in a garage back in Logan County.

If Wiki had a lead on Petey Thunkle, maybe some good could come of this. A win tonight might get her back on track, and if nothing else, maybe they could put all focus on the shuttle saboteur. Catch them and all the other disappointments would've been worth it. Maybe.

Free school. A job afterward. Most importantly, save the farm.

Yet a nagging voice in the back of her mind—one that sounded suspiciously like Harlow—whispered, "If that's the way you earn a position at the best tech company in the world, would you *really* deserve it?"

"So . . . what you got?" Leen asked, her breath puffing as she settled into a chilly chair before Petey's workstation.

Wiki woke up her ThunklePad tablet and did a hard, whole-hand swipe that flung the photos from the tablet display to the big monitors on Petey's workstation. "Did you note the time we entered the Egg?"

"Yep. Nine forty-five p.m."

"Keep that in mind and start a stopwatch."

Leen had no clue why but also no desire to argue. She pulled down her goggles, tapped her gauntlet, and a stopwatch started counting in her Heads-Up Display. She raised the goggles to the top of her head. "Okay."

Wiki motioned to the photos they'd taken. "Look at the timestamps?"

Leen did, still confused. "They are stamping the time."

"Think about the first night we were alone here. We took one hundred and forty-two pictures. Carefully. Over two hours of photographing." Wiki swiped through the photos, first all the way to last, the timestamps confirming what she said.

"Okay?"

"Do you remember when we got back to our room, it didn't feel so late? Definitely not like it was close to midnight."

"So what?" Usually, it was Leen who rambled. Wiki never took this long to make a point. Did she have one? Leen couldn't tell.

Wiki said, "Then there's the milk!"

Oh, this was going off the rails now. "Wik, I don't know what you're saying."

Wiki was fidgety, pacing. "Hang on, hang on. What's your stopwatch say?"

Leen checked her goggles. "Eight minutes, fifty-four seconds."

Wiki drew shapes in the air with her index finger, like she was marking a whiteboard visible only to her. Were they numbers or letters, or a magic spell? Leen didn't know for sure. It was super weird.

Wiki mumbled, "Three more minutes should do it." Then she got loud again. "The milk. It spoiled."

"You left it out."

"True. But it's as cold as a refrigerator in here, so that shouldn't have mattered."

"Unless it was about to go bad already."

"Except it wasn't. Britney had a carton with the same expiration date. Her milk was fine."

"Why are we spending so much time on milk?" This was getting very frustrating.

Wiki said, "Remember the note Petey left behind?"

"Not really. You're the one with the memory, sooooo . . ."

Wiki recited: "'Anna, My Bae, If you're reading this, then I have missed my twenty-four-hour window and that's way longer than I intended.' It sounds weird. Why not just say 'I missed my twenty-four-hour window'? 'Why the 'longer than I intended' part?"

"He's wordy."

Wiki wrung her hands. "What's the stopwatch say?"

"Twelve minutes, three seconds."

"Perfect. Stop it now. And tell me what time we came in here."

Leen did as told and repeated the time she'd stated earlier. "Nine forty-five according to the clock on Anna's desk."

"Follow me."

Wiki broke the seal on the Egg, letting in some welcome warm air, and they walked the tunnel back to Anna Thunkle's office. Emerging from the Egg portal, Wiki said, "Check Anna's clock."

Leen, over all of it, did as told, and . . .

No.

Wait.

No.

The clock read 9:46 p.m., just one minute more than when they'd entered the Egg.

"That's—" Leen almost said *impossible*. She was from Logan County though, so she knew better.

Wiki said, "Now do you get it?"

Yeah. She got it.

Whoa.

Leen insisted they test it a few more times using the formula $x \div 12 = y$.

Where x is time inside the Egg, and y is time outside the Egg.

They did twelve minutes inside, which equaled one minute outside again. Then thirty-six minutes inside, which amounted to three minutes outside. All the way up to an hour inside for five minutes of time out in Anna's office.

It was relative, of course. If you were inside the Egg, it didn't *feel* like time moved differently. How did that work, though?

And what did it mean for the missing Petey Thunkle?

Wiki said, "Petey's letter. He wouldn't have left that if he didn't think he might have a problem eventually. Also—" Wiki stopped herself. She was about to say the Interstellar-Z shuttle was a big clue but couldn't quite explain that one yet. "Also, we should look at this workspace a bit differently than we have before. Do your goggles have an ultraviolet setting?"

"Of course." Leen flipped them down and started a scan. "What are we looking for?"

"Fingerprints in weird places."

So Leen searched under the desks, along the safety railings, behind the monitors. There were plenty of fingerprints all around, though nothing that raised any alarms.

Until Leen got back to Petey's desk. The luminescent green orbs Leen had spotted all over the place were concentrated in one spot, emitting a dusty, speckled glow under the UV light.

"That mug"—she pointed—"with all the pens and pencils. Only one of the pens—the fancy looking PeteyTech one—is covered in fingerprints."

Wiki grabbed the pen to examine it more closely. It barely budged, yet something inside the mug clicked the way a switch does, and the bright white lights of the Egg turned an ominous electric blue. She said, "We might have a problem."

"Let's go!" Leen ran for the catwalk, but that was no longer an option—the catwalk had detached from the tunnel. It retracted in on itself, drawing closer to the workstation, as did all the other catwalks leading to the walkway along the Egg's perimeter.

As if all the suddenly moving parts inside the Egg weren't alarming enough, the floor of the workstation was shifting. Those uneven grooves that they'd always had to be careful not to trip over weren't just bad craftsmanship. It was a partially ajar hatch.

Now, it yawned all the way open and something else glowing with strange electric blue light rose slowly to the girls' level.

Leen scooted around to Wiki until they were shoulder to shoulder. If there were going to be disintegrated, at least they'd be together.

Wiki, though concerned for their safety, became more curious than afraid as the object ascended into view.

It was . . .

Wiki groaned. Unamused.

They were already in an egg-shaped room, at a workstation called the Chicken. And rising from the floor beneath the Chicken was *another* egg.

Really, Petey Thunkle?

The man seemed downright insufferable.

This new glowing egg pulsed. Bright blue, dull blue, plain white, repeat. When it was at its dimmest, Leen made out a fine seam that ran along its curved top.

Once the little egg was completely clear of its hidden hutch, a message flashed on every monitor on Petey's desk. It read: *Execute Return Sequence?*

The girls eyed each other, then the little egg. The workstation was an island in the center of the big egg, an island they couldn't escape with no catwalks. They'd have to do *something* to even get out of here. Also, the word *return* offered the slimmest hope. Didn't it?

They nodded at each other, and Leen hit two keys on the keyboard: Y and Enter.

That's when the lightning started.

15

These Are Not the Geniuses
You're Looking For

Electric bolts snapped between the exterior of the small egg
and the interior of the big egg. Wiki and Leen took shelter
under the nearest worktable while the sizzling maelstrom
scorched the air. It lasted maybe ten seconds, though it felt
like ten years and had Wiki wondering, *What if ten years
passed outside of the Egg?* They were messing with *time* after
all. As quickly as it started, the lightning barrage ended.

"Look." Leen pointed.

The seam atop the tiny egg widened, opened like a suitcase, the sides spreading far apart on concealed hinges until
they butted the floor. Inside the small egg was a hole.

In the air.

A portal.

The girls could barely make it out from their hiding spot,

but the rim of the portal floated at roughly eye level and wavered like asphalt fumes on a hot day.

Two arms thrust up and out of the portal like bunny ears poking from a rabbit's hole, making the girls yelp.

Those arms grabbed handholds protruding from the split interior of the egg for leverage, then a head and torso and hips and legs followed. The man, whom the girls didn't recognize at first because they'd never seen him look quite how he looked, scrambled from the portal fully, then collapsed sideways onto the floor.

Pushing up to his feet, he stumbled around on wobbly legs. His outfit was strange, reminiscent of Mama and Daddy's Fry High School yearbook photos from a lot of years ago. He wore a too-big burgundy sweatsuit made of glossy, fuzzy material Mama called "velour." There was a huge gold

chain dangling over his chest. He wore a New York Yankees cap that fit like an oversized motorcycle helmet, hiding his eyes. A scraggly beard covered his usually smooth face.

Petey Thunkle looked very different from the photos on Anna's desk.

From his loose jacket, he produced a device that resembled an extra large ThunklePhone. The screen glimmered with scrolling code before the device belched a plume of gray, ozone-scented smoke and went dark.

The portal vanished. The egg resealed itself. The lights throughout the entire structure returned to their normal bright white hue, and the catwalks slowly extended to their original positions, allowing them a way out. Thank goodness.

Petey teetered on shaky legs, glancing up and around as if unsure where he was. Spinning, he spotted the girls, his expression shifting from shocked to something like—

It took a moment for Wiki to read, simply because she often interpreted facial tics based on what was happening in the moment. If the conversation was about someone's sick pet and a person's face went slack, that was sadness. It made sense. What was on Petey's face when his eyes landed on Leen came off as . . . *shame*? Which didn't make any sense.

Did it?

What did he have to be ashamed of? He's the one who told Anna to put them on the case.

He said, "Wiki and Leen Ellison? What are *you*—?"

His eyes rolled back so all they saw were the whites, and he fainted.

Awesome.

"Petey sweetie," Anna said, lightly patting his cheeks. "Petey, wake up!"

Thankfully Petey Thunkle was stick thin, so Wiki and Leen were able to lug him from the Egg with a lot of teamwork and only a bit of strain. They'd plonked him on the couch in Anna's office.

Pettygrew was present when the girls and Petey emerged from the Egg seeking help. The assistant brought Anna right away. She'd entered rubbing her stomach and immediately drenched her blouse in tears. She dedicated herself to patting her husband's cheeks and repeating his name. "Petey. Petey."

The girls suggested he might need a doctor, but Anna insisted they give him a few moments. Sure enough, he groaned his way to consciousness. "Ugghhhh. I just wanna sleep."

"Petey, are you okay? Where have you been?"

"I was with me." His eyes remained shut. "It was a lovely time."

Leen mumble-quoted his words. "'I was with me.'" To Wiki, she said, "He came outta that egg a cuckoo bird."

Only Wiki didn't think so.

Anna said, "I did as you asked and got the geniuses from Logan County. They were everything you said they'd be."

Finally his eyelids parted. He spotted Wiki and Leen immediately. "Hey, girls!"

"Hi," they said back.

Petey winced and rubbed his temples like he had a massive headache, then swung his feet to the floor, sweeping his gaze across the room as if looking for someone else. "Where are they?" he asked.

Anna seemed confused. "Who?"

"The team I told you to get in my letter." He yelled, "Otto, Sheed, come out! I'm awake."

Leen's stomach fell all the way to the lobby. Wiki's heart turned as cold as the Egg. She recalled Petey's letter, word for word:

> . . . I trust you, sweet sugarplum, to decipher what and who is needed here. You know where we grew up. You remember how strange it could be there. Well, there's a pair of genius problem-solvers there who can help. They're the best at what they do. Find them. They can bring me home.

Wiki thought, *He wasn't talking about us.*

He wanted the Legendary Alston Boys. He thinks they're better.

Petey, startled, shot a questioning look to Anna.

She said, "You told me to find the best. Of all the strange happenings back home, these girls were the ones the *Logan*

County Gazette credited with the most cases solved, the most people saved. My research said *they're the best.*"

Petey winced again, not from a headache. "Are they, though?"

Anna scoffed. White-hot rage rose in Wiki and she bit her tongue to keep from saying stuff that would've gotten her grounded back home. Leen wished she'd brought along Dewey and some of her other drones to unleash on this man.

Leen snapped, "We brought you home! Not the Alston Boys! *Us!*"

Petey scrambled to find the right words that would somehow make his insult not be insulting. "I'm not saying you aren't good, but some things don't make it into the research. If Anna found you through the reports of your work, that's wonderful. Thank you. I only meant, with Otto and Sheed, maybe there's stuff they've done that hasn't made the papers. Stuff none of you would know about. Stuff that makes them . . . better *suited* than you."

Wiki clenched her fists.

Petey looked like he wanted to leap over the couch in terror. "Hey, no need to be angry. I'm only trying to explain what you may not understand."

"Enough, Peter!" Anna's hands rested on her baby bump like a shield. "Those girls don't need your explanation, and neither do I. I made the right call, and they brought you home. What you *can* explain is what happened inside your egg to cause this mess. *And why are you dressed like an old-school rapper?*"

Petey's eyes bounced between the three of them, panicky. He placed his hand on his forehead as if checking his own temperature. "Whoo! I feel faint again."

Anna leapt forward, clutching a handful of his velour collar. "Do not faint. Talk!"

"I love you, Anna." Gently, he caressed her hand, then pried her fingers loose. "But I can't. I'm sorry."

Petey Thunkle stood, walked toward the exit. "I'm heading up to our residence to change and get some rest. Now that I'm back, things will move quickly. I know you want more from me, but I can't give more to you. Thank you, Wiki and Leen. Though I may have envisioned something different, I really do mean that."

He left them. Unsatisfied.

Anna said, "I'm sorry, girls. What he said was uncalled for."

Leen, having experienced one disappointment too many, said, "Maybe he's right."

"No," Wiki said. Never believing that the Legendary Alston Boys were better than them. Not for one second.

Well, maybe for one or two seconds after Petey Thunkle said it. But that was like how anyone felt in the second or two after someone said a mean thing. They said it—even if they didn't know they were being mean, though sometimes they knew full well—because they wanted you to think they're right. It'd be like if someone said don't think about purple crocodiles, then immediately asked what color crocodile you were thinking of.

People could put junk in your head as easily as they tossed it in a trash can. Don't be their trash can.

Leen always had a harder time with that than Wiki though. Leen's tics and tells were screaming, *I'm not good enough.* For what or for whom, Wiki didn't know. It didn't matter. In this regard, her supersmart inventor sister was wrong.

The tricky part was convincing *her.*

"Leen—" Wiki said.

Leen cut her off. "I think maybe I want to go home now."

Anna's head whipped their way. "No. You don't mean that."

Wiki told Anna, "You got your husband back. Would you really care that much if we left?"

Anna nodded while looking hurt. "That is a fair question. Dr. Burr's message about the burden I placed on you girls was not lost on me. Yes, I *would* care if you left Cosmos Camp early. I would blame myself and Petey for such a tragic turn of events—maybe him more so, though I know I'm not without fault. I do understand what it's like to miss home. I miss Logan more often than you think. Girls, take a quick trip with me."

"Not back into the Egg?" Wiki asked, alarmed. They still needed to talk about the time anomaly in there.

130

"Oh no. We're going to the twenty-fourth floor. I think you'll like it there."

Neither Wiki nor Leen were convinced they would—PeteyTech surprises hadn't been of the super-fun variety so far. But the twenty-fourth floor was on the way to the first, so a quick stop couldn't hurt. Hopefully.

In the hall, Pettygrew's vacuum motor ran ceaselessly, though there was no mess to clean. Her holographic facade crackled into view. She wrung her hands nervously. "Mr. Thunkle is back. Yay?"

"Somewhat yay, Pettygrew. Keep an eye on him. He's a little shaky. Unless he requires medical attention, don't call me. I'm not in the mood to deal with him further right now."

The hologram shuddered. "That's chilly. But . . . understood."

Pettygrew winked away and motored down the corridor to carry out Anna's orders. As she zoomed from sight, the elevator dinged. They climbed aboard, and Anna pressed twenty-four. A quick trip but much farther than just the twenty stories between there and Anna's office. When the elevator doors opened, they opened onto Fry, Virginia. Main Street to be exact.

The elevator had taken them home.

16

Homecoming

This place shouldn't be here.

At first, Wiki feared this was *another* unexplained time-space phenomenon taking place under the roof of PeteyTech. How else could they be back in Fry, Virginia? Their hometown. A place they knew better than any other.

Wiki blinked and let her brain do its thing, pinging all the inconsistencies her initial panic had her overlooking. Her mind overlaid her last memories of Fry's Main Street—the real Main Street from a few weeks ago—onto the scene in front of her.

The bulbs in the Lopsided Furniture Company sign were wrong, too modern, and the paint was a shade too dark. Nice Dream Ice Cream Shop was still here, even though it had become Riches Brew coffee shop months ago. There was no

Rorrim Mirror Emporium—which was probably for the best, all things considered.

Since this was not the real Fry Main Street, what *was* it?

Anna stepped from the elevator onto the asphalt road running between the stores on either side of the street. There were people here, appearing to browse shop windows, though their expressions were bored and annoyed. They wore clothes similar to the everyday Fry resident—work boots, jeans, flannel shirts—but they also wore lanyards with their PeteyTech IDs dangling on their chests.

The street ran roughly the length of an entire PeteyTech Tower floor before stopping abruptly at a wall that had been painted to look like more of the town stretched into the distance.

Overhead, the ceiling was curved and painted to resemble a blue springtime sky with puffy plastic clouds dangling from cables.

Leen craned her neck, taking in the engineering aspects of this floor. What it would take to give such a reasonable impression of the street they knew so well. It reminded her of amusement parks that could make you believe you were walking through a different country or a fantasy kingdom. Not difficult but very costly.

Or not. If you were one of the richest people in the world.

Anna said, "The accomplishments of PeteyTech have

allowed me some privileges, you might say. This is one of them."

Wiki, skeptical, said, "Because you miss home so much?"

"No."

Wiki appreciated that bit of honesty.

Anna waddled along. "Though I've come to enjoy this floor more than I anticipated, it wasn't created for me."

She stopped before a familiar storefront that no longer existed in actual Fry, Virginia. Archie's Hardware. The store Anna's father had owned back home for many years.

Tugging open the double doors, Anna drowned out the sound of the chimes by yelling, "Dad! You in here?"

"Hey there!" Mr. Archie rounded some shelves, carrying a cardboard box of paint rollers. He placed the box on the counter, trotted to Anna, kissed her check, then crouched until he was eye level with her bulging stomach. He spoke softly then. "How's my little blueberry doing in there? You're having a good day, I hope."

"Blueberry?" Leen asked.

Only then did Mr. Archie notice them. His grin stretched. "Wiki and Leen Ellison? It's so good to see you girls. What a surprise! How's your mom, dad, and Percy?"

"They're fine!" Wiki was overjoyed to see him. It'd been a long time.

Leen said, "Percy really misses you, sir. He complains

134

all the time about having to drive to Richmond for a decent hardware store."

Mr. Archie's face got a little sad over that. "I do miss being there for Fry. But I can't miss welcoming the newest Thunkle into the world."

Wiki asked, "Why do you call the baby 'blueberry'?"

"That would be my fault," Anna said. "At one of our early doctor appointments we got to hear her heartbeat, and they told us she was very small then, the size of a blueberry. So I kept referring to her as 'blueberry.' Then Dad started calling her 'blueberry.' Then Petey joined in. She's much bigger now, but she hasn't quite outgrown the name."

Leen said it again: "Blueberry. I like it."

She stepped farther into the store, radiating enthusiasm that was more common when she wasn't at Cosmos Camp. "I like this place too. Why does it exist, though?"

Mr. Archie joined Leen and led them on a tour of a near-perfect reconstruction of the chaotic hardware store. "I had a tough time when I first got here. Not much to do, Wasn't allowed into many of the areas because the company does a lot of secret work. Got bored, and it made me real sad."

Anna said, "Petey asked what we could do to make Dad more comfortable."

Wiki could barely believe what she was hearing. "This is what you came up with?"

"We had a spare floor."

Of course Wiki was calculating the effort this must have taken and couldn't help but think how that effort could've been directed elsewhere in a way that might help people who maybe needed it more. Yet to see hints of joy on Leen's face as she browsed goods she was likely already imagining into more marvelous forms eased some judgment.

Some. Not all. The people roaming the sidewalks outside . . .

Wiki asked, "Are those PeteyTech employees on the street pretending they're from Fry?"

"We wanted it to be as real as possible," Anna said, missing the harshness in Wiki's tone.

"You hired them specifically for this?"

"No. They're scientists, mathematicians, and engineers. We simply allotted them time to spend part of their shift here."

Leen's head snapped toward Anna, some of her joy seeping away.

These supersmart people who'd dedicated their lives to science now spent part of their workday fake-shopping so Anna and her dad could pretend they were somewhere else?

Something in Mr. Archie's posture—a slight slumping of his shoulders, the way he now looked at his shoes—suggested he understood what a waste of talent this was.

Anna asked, "How are you feeling now, girls?"

"Great!" said Wiki. She stared at Leen hard.

Leen got the message and said a passable "Awesome."

"Excellent. I knew this might cheer you up. Ready to return to camp?"

"Can't wait," the girls said together.

Wiki may have been rushing to get some privacy so they could talk, but Leen really meant it. Partially because the wonder of this floor had worn off. Mostly, she wanted to go because she still had the busted device Petey had dropped when he fainted, and she wanted a closer look.

Back in their quarters, reeling from all that had happened and unclear about what it meant for the rest of their days at Cosmos Camp, there was still one more thing to do before bed—if sleep came at all.

Each of them screwed in their ThunklePod earbuds. They opened the ThunkleTime app on their ThunklePhones, and Wiki initiated the necessary group call.

The ringing chime sounded for a few seconds before a neat four-square grid filled each of their screens. Wiki's and Leen's faces were visible in the top squares, and the bottom two displayed their hometown rivals . . . the Legendary Alston Boys of Logan County.

Sheed Alston was in the bottom left square, taking the

call from his dad's condo in downtown Fry and habitually picking his afro. He said, "Hey, Leen."

"Hey," she said. Gruff. Unlike their usual grossly sweet greeting.

"What's wrong? Camp going okay?"Sheed asked.

"It is not!" Wiki said. "We're hoping you can help us understand why that is the case, Otto."

Otto Alston, taking the call from the boys' room at their grandma's, appeared in the bottom right square looking as ridiculously perplexed as ever. "Huh?"

"Petey Thunkle," Wiki said. "How do you know him? *Why* do you know him?"

The boys got suspiciously quiet. No denial (so they did know Petey), no quick response (so they didn't want the Epic Ellisons to know). Wiki was losing her patience. "Look! I'm not in the mood to pick you two apart like I normally do. Petey Thunkle mentioned you by name. I know he's from Logan County, but that doesn't explain why the richest man on earth knows you two."

Still quiet. Still nothing.

Leen said, "Fellas, if it's got something to do with time travel, we're pretty sure he's into that, so you might as well spill."

Sheed stopped picking his afro. Otto looked like he might hyperventilate.

Wiki said, "Octavius Alston!"

"All right, all right. Dag!" Otto said. "Sheed, you cool with this?"

Sheed nodded. "I don't like secrets."

"Me neither," said Leen, her fiercest glare aimed at her unofficial boyfriend.

Otto took a deep breath. "It happened last year, on the last day of summer. And what you need to understand is, first of all, Grandma's teacup-pig calendar lied . . ."

17

Previously on Logan County Adventures . . .

"Leen! Wiki!" Sheed interrupted Otto to ask, "Can you set your phones up side by side for proper dramatization?"

The girls shrugged and propped their phones on Wiki's headboard as requested, which shifted the screen orientation and gave the odd impression that Otto and Sheed were standing beside each other as they would in real-life Logan County.

Then, Otto started the most bonkers story the girls had ever heard. "Like I was saying, last summer, on the last day, I kinda sorta goofed up."

Sheed leaned into his screen. "He was salty because you two had more Keys to the City than us, and he wished we had more time to get more keys, and this dude who wasn't a dude tricked Otto into freezing time!"

Otto, tight-lipped and staring, breathed really hard,

annoyed breaths. "There was nothing dramatic about that. If you're just going to blurt it . . ."

Sheed picked his hair. "Sorry, sorry. Go on."

Otto said, "When I froze time—"

"You gonna tell them about the time traveler? And the Clock Watchers? And the Missed Opportunity? And the Time Sucks?"

Otto shouted, "I cannot orate under these conditions, Sheed!"

"Sorry, sorry. Go on."

Wiki shot a look at Leen, her lips curled in a *what is this?* expression that Leen could only shrug off.

Sheed finally allowed Otto to get to it. He told of a being named Mr. Flux, who tricked Otto into freezing time with a magic camera, an act that drew the attention of a time traveler from the future named TimeStar and unleashed a race

of people called Clock Watchers from a parallel dimension. While none of them were strangers to the weirdly improbable happenings in Logan County, this tale was shaping up to be quite a bit weirder than their usual Logan County shenanigans.

Otto said, "We found out Mr. Flux was actually the angry, vengeful manifestation of Missed Opportunity, created when a young version of Petey Thunkle refused to do more with his passion for science."

Sheed interrupted with useful information. "The Petey Thunkle we knew before all that happened was different from who he is now. He didn't have any confidence. He wasn't rich. He was a clerk at Archie's Hardware."

Otto said, "When Leen helped the original Petey fix some time-travel tech, we used it to go back so older, no-confidence Petey could talk his younger self into pursuing their dreams. That act defeated Mr. Flux."

"And changed everything," Sheed said.

"When we returned to the present, Petey was the guy you know: successful, rich, looks like he's done a lot of good."

"Looks can be deceiving!" Wiki said.

Leen's response was more thoughtful. "I helped the original version of Petey fix a time-travel device from the future?"

"Sure did. You were awesome," Sheed said, then added, in his trying-to-sound-smooth, fake deep voice, "like always."

Otto made gagging motions on his screen, but Leen barely noticed.

In the Alstons' story, she *sounded* awesome. Too bad she had absolutely no memory of it. She'd love to *feel* awesome. Especially lately.

Wiki, for her part in this, felt alarming familiarity. The things the Alstons said—time freezing, this Mr. Flux guy—she now had vague recollections of. She never remembered things *vaguely*!

Most of her memories, like 99.9999 percent, were crisp and subject to instant recall. The events Otto and Sheed detailed were different. A hazier version of other things she'd sensed were a little off in the world these days. She had a bad feeling about why. "You guys and Petey are the only ones who remember how the world used to be when Petey had no confidence?"

The boys nodded.

"Have there been big changes other than Petey making himself rich?"

"There were no flying cars before."

Well, there still weren't a ton. Mostly they were in bigger cities, like New York and Los Angeles. "What else?"

"I think ThunklePhones used to be called something else." Otto stroked his chin, his brow furrowed like he was struggling to find his words. "I can't remember the name now, though. Like there's fog in my brain."

143

Wiki felt a sharp pain in her temple. Then, she said something that felt funny in her mouth. "iPhones?"

Otto snapped his fingers. "That sounds familiar."

Wiki's head pounded. "There are other things too."

Strange words and phrases floated in and out of her mind, sometimes crashing with very familiar terms. ThunkleTube smashed into something called *You . . . Tube*? The Thupotle restaurant that Uncle Percy got his chicken and rice bowls from collided with *Chipotle*, which made a lot more sense. In two parallel thoughts—two parallel *memories*—Wiki remembered using *Google* to search for something on the web at the same time she recalled using Thoogle. It all sounded like nonsense, yet each weird word mix triggered throbbing pain that made it impossible for her to ignore. The farther back she thought, the harder it became to distinguish between BEFORE poor Petey and AFTER rich Petey.

She groaned and managed to say, "He's changed so much."

Otto and Sheed looked puzzled. Leen was concerned for her sister. She said, "Hey, guys, we'll call back later. Bye."

Leen ended the call, then made her sister lie down. "You don't look so good, Wik."

Maybe it was spending so much time in the Egg or being too close to Petey's portal when he returned or simply hearing the truth from the Alstons that triggered it—she didn't know. But it was like having one of the nightmares she'd experienced over the last year while still awake. The different versions of everything, things that were lost to everyone else, still existed in her head, and when they clashed with their new versions—the Petey Thunkle versions—she suffered.

Not just her, though.

Last summer they weren't there. At all. Now people are zipping around the sky like dragonflies. I'm telling you, something changed.

The podcast Mama had been playing on their ride to Cosmos Camp—the woman in the mental hospital who remembered that last summer PeteyTech flying cars weren't a thing. She wasn't losing touch with reality . . . she was *remembering the truth.*

How many other people were like Wiki? Like that woman from the podcast? How many people knew the world wasn't what it used to be and were being dismissed while Petey Thunkle got more rich and more powerful?

". . . while he steals?"

Leen said, "Steals what?"

Wiki's headache was so intense, she didn't realize she was saying some stuff while only thinking other stuff.

To Leen it sounded like the time Uncle Percy had a real high fever from the flu and started seeing dancing unicorns.

That was scary because he needed strong medicine to feel better. "I'm going to get Dr. Burr!"

Wiki grabbed her sleeve. "I'm fine. It's passing. We gotta do something about Petey, though. He's a thief."

"What did he steal?"

"The past. And the future. Everything."

Leen shook her head, not understanding.

"For one, your shuttle idea." Wiki sat up in her bunk, her anger surpassing her pain. "You designed the anti-friction coating on the Interstellar-Z."

"He . . . ?" Leen said. "I . . . did?"

"You did. Based on what Otto and Sheed said, you might've been the one to help him crack time travel too."

Leen flopped on her bunk, trying not to get too caught up on the I-designed-stuff-I-don't-remember part. She pieced together all they'd seen with all they'd heard. "Petey's taking good ideas from the present to his younger self so it seems like he came up with them first?"

"Not good ideas. The best ideas. The most popular ones. The ones that made other people rich. It's nearly the perfect crime too. Only a few people in the whole world have a sense of it. It's making me wonder something."

"Something like . . . ?"

"What if the thing trying to sabotage Petey's rocket launch knows too?"

18

This Plan Is Trash

Sleeping was hard that night, and the next day's Cosmos Camp exercises were harder. Wiki's head continued its low throbbing, making it difficult to concentrate. Britney, Sierra, and Kelvin noticed. Especially Kelvin, who pulled her aside before lunch to ask, "Ellison, are you okay?"

No. She was not okay. Everything, including the very building they occupied at the moment, was a lie. That was not an answer Kelvin would likely accept or want.

Britney and Sierra worked on a vegetation experiment that was meant to be produced in zero gravity, like real astronauts did. They kept cutting their eyes toward Kelvin and Wiki, though their tics indicated they thought they were being sly about it.

Wiki said, "Didn't sleep so well. A little tired is all."

147

Kelvin's head bobbed. "Because if there was something going on, you can tell us. You should tell us. We're your team."

The way he leaned in and whispered when he said that suggested he didn't really mean tell *the team*. He meant tell *him*. That was weird. She said, "Errr, okay."

Wiki got back to tending her zero-gravity lettuce but was less interested in the end goal of all this. Being on flight crew, or mission control, seemed less motivating when it was all being done in a place built on stolen ideas.

Leen, on the other hand, was not getting a concerned vibe from Red Team while they worked on their space cucumbers. It felt more like attacks. Harlow wouldn't let Leen's rocket-design fail go, and there was no way to convince her that Leen had designed a key component of the rocket siting on the launchpad—not that she wanted to impress Harlow, Pierre, and Chest anymore. In the true memory Wiki detailed, the mean kids had flocked to Leen when she'd won them the design contest. They'd only been friendly when her work benefited them. They'd used her. No one needs friends like that.

She felt a strong urge to show them up, though. Let them see how epic she really was.

Those were petty thoughts. Mama would've said, "You're not taking the high road, Evangeleen."

Mean people made the low-road way more appealing.

Now that she could see the kinds of people her teammates were, and the kind of person Petey Thunkle was, it drew her attention to their Cosmos Camp leader.

What had PeteyTech stolen from Dr. Burr? What if she was one of the people—like Wiki—who recognized the truth of all the company's accomplishments?

What if that knowledge made her want revenge?

The shape-shifting saboteur had been in *her* office, on *her* computer.

At lunch, Red Team switched tables without notifying Leen. Wiki noticed and waved Leen over to Blue Team's table, but Leen declined. She wanted the alone time to think about all she'd learned. And to watch Dr. Burr.

The doctor also ate alone, swiping through who knows what on her ThunklePad and writing various notes in a spiral notebook she always kept with her.

Dr. Burr didn't seem to interact with any other people, except for Ally the custodian, who often passed Dr. Burr's table for a brief conversation and to take the doctor's tray, saving her a visit from the Sani-Bot that took everyone else's tray.

Wait.

Leen had observed this ritual most days since camp started. Dr. Burr with her ThunklePad, scribbling her notes, Ally rolling her cart over, Dr. Burr passing off her tray. No big deal, right?

Except things that weren't a big deal yesterday were a big deal now.

Before Ally took Dr. Burr's tray, the doctor repositioned her ThunklePad so that it blocked the view of her notebook. It was quick. Almost unnoticeable.

Leen left her seat, dropped her nearly full tray off with the Sani-Bot, and joined Dr. Burr uninvited. "Hello."

"Ellison." Dr. Burr fidgeted, glancing around the room as if someone were playing a joke on her. "Can I help you?"

"This afternoon we'll be doing more shuttle control training, right? I was wondering if the ship can do barrel rolls?"

"Barrel rolls? Why would you want to do barrel rolls in a shuttle?"

"Why would you not?"

Dr. Burr heavy sighed. "Traditional shuttles do have the ability to roll. In fact, depending on how they reenter the atmosphere, the maneuver may be necessary. But they aren't stunt planes. You see—"

Leen kept a pen in her jumpsuit pocket. She removed it and made a show of checking her pockets for scrap paper. "Oh shoot. I want to take notes but don't have anything to write on. Would it be okay if I—?"

Leen motioned to the doctor's notebook.

Caught up in her mini lecture, Dr. Burr didn't object.

Leen flipped the notebook open. First noticing the

ragged scraps of torn edges crammed in the spiral binding, then confirming what she'd suspected once she knew what to look for.

For all those days of note-taking, the pages before Leen at that moment were blank. Every note gone.

Or, most likely, transported elsewhere by Ally.

This revelation came with new questions.

1) Why?

2) Who the heck *was* Ally?

Wiki said, "So we're tailing the janitor?"

It was after lights-out. The girls were in their all-black sneaking clothes, but until that moment, Wiki wasn't sure where they'd be sneaking. She never wanted to return to the Egg unless they were going to destroy it, and no way Petey Thunkle was going to allow that. She got queasy thinking he, at that very moment, might be planning another trip to take stolen ideas to the past. Queasier to think they were powerless to stop it. In every version of reality her memories presented, rich people like Petey Thunkle did what they wanted.

So this idea of targeting someone who wasn't rich . . . didn't seem so cool.

"Yes," Leen confirmed. "We're tailing the janitor."

"Why?"

"Because Dr. Burr gives her trash."

Wiki didn't have a great way to respond. "I thought we were focusing on the saboteur."

"Yes. We are."

"By tailing the janitor?"

"Wik. The trash had notes."

Leen didn't always relay details in ways that people might find coherent. She knew that. It's the reason Wiki did most of the talking. Since Wiki couldn't tell herself the things that were in Leen's head, these sorts of conversations were tougher than most. Leen resorted to "Can you just trust me for once?"

Wiki looked aghast. "I've always trusted you. Since the day we were born. Do you think I don't?"

"I don't know what I think anymore." It was the truest thing she'd said in a while. At least in *this* version of Petey Thunkle's world.

"We tail her," Wiki said, "but we don't do anything that can get her in trouble unless we know she and Dr. Burr are *definitely* doing something wrong. We stay invisible."

Leen tugged on a black ski mask and new stealth goggles she'd been dying to try. "Let's go."

19

Mom?! Wait. What?!

They found Ally cleaning the atrium between the Cosmos Camp training hangar and the PeteyTech Tower. The girls stuck to the shadows, hiding behind support columns and large potted plants so they wouldn't be seen while their target went about her duties. The custodian pushed her cart near the gigantic windowpanes along the building's face. She spotted some fingerprints and stopped to clean the glass. Two spritzes of cleaner, five circular wipes with a cloth, and she moved on. Nothing unusual.

A few more steps and she came upon a discarded chewing gum wrapper. She removed her dustpan and broom, collecting the paper with two quick, precise sweeps. This triggered a Wiki memory from two weeks ago when she'd glanced Ally performing the exact motion sweeping up a crumpled napkin in the cafeteria.

Maybe the custodian was a creature of habit? Like Uncle Percy clipping his toenails every Tuesday during his favorite singing competition, *The Thunkle Voice*.

Wiki winced from a sharp pain in her temple. *The Voice*. Just *The Voice*. Another Petey change! Uggggh!

They ducked behind some lobby couches while Ally strolled by. Leen said, "I wonder if the note Dr. Burr slipped her is still in her bin."

"Doubt it. That was hours ago," Wiki said. "But she doesn't take the bin home, right? Maybe it's in her pocket or a purse."

Leen nodded. The logic was sound. "We follow her until her shift ends, then see what she does."

Only, her shift didn't end. The girls followed her for three hours, which meant from the first they'd seen of Ally that morning, she'd been working nearly eighteen hours. A long, long time. They didn't work that long on their family farm.

This seemed . . . odd.

Ally didn't stop to drink water. Maybe because she didn't stop to drink water was the reason she didn't stop to pee, but Wiki and Leen hadn't had much water and they both needed a pee break that required them to catch up to Ally, who was never too far away. She'd continued her route until she looped back to the Cosmos Camp hangar.

Not only had she cleaned the whole time, but she had

also hummed. Three songs. Not songs the girls recognized, but Wiki had clocked a loop there too. When Ally started over, the songs were note perfect. No variation.

People weren't usually this precise. Get a person to sign their name ten times, each signature will have slight variations. The only way a song sounded the same every time was if you replayed the same recording. Ally hummed like a recording.

Wiki said, "It's weird, but if she goes through another cleaning loop, I don't think I can take it."

Leen felt yet another of her ideas falling flat. Maybe there wasn't anything to be seen here.

Ally made an abrupt turn, angling her cart toward a supply closet. The girls hung back as she opened the door, pushed her cart in as if to park it for the night, then stepped inside with it, sparing a quick left-to-right glance to make sure the coast was clear.

The custodian closed herself into the closet.

Wiki said, "That's definitely worth investigating."

They tiptoed to the closet. Leen tested the knob—not locked—then nudged the door open. It was a *deep* closet. Lots of shelves. Lots of supplies. Ally's custodial cart parked to the side. But no Ally.

Leen adjusted her goggles and scanned the back wall.

"Is it a door?" Wiki asked.

"You know it."

The locking mechanism—a false bottle of toilet bowl cleaner—wasn't particularly well hidden. A quarter turn of the container triggered the pneumatics that opened the hidden passage.

Was this another Egg? Something worse?

What they found was . . . Well, they didn't know.

It was Ally in a glass vat, her body curving/warping/morphing in a way they'd seen before.

She was the shape-shifting creature that had been altering the shuttle codes from Dr. Burr's office.

What kind of creature was that?

Was the vat a place she rested at night, like a vampire returning to its coffin at sunrise? Did it recharge her?

"Ally is the saboteur?" Leen said.

A shadow fell over them.

"You've got it all wrong, girls. Our team isn't sabotaging PeteyTech. We're trying to save it. Whether or not Petey Thunkle deserves our help is another question."

The girls faced Dr. Burr.

She blocked their way out of the closet. And she wasn't alone.

Someone tall and lanky stood behind her, draped in shadow. He said, "We gotta tell them, Mom!"

Mom?

Kelvin stepped into the light. Then the lights went out.

Ally.

Whatever she was, she'd slipped from her vat, and her shape-shifting hands morphed into opaque sacks that covered the girls' heads so they couldn't see or scream. Other parts of Ally snapped around their wrists and legs like shifting sand they couldn't shake off, binding them. No matter how much they wiggled, bucked, bounced, or kicked . . . they were stuck. But also in motion, being carried away by Ally.

To whatever Dr. Burr had planned for them next.

Dr. Burr's voice remained soothing during the trip. "We're not going to hurt you, girls. This is just a conversation."

Isn't that the thing someone would say if they were going to hurt you, though?

Despite being unable to see, the compass in Wiki's head pointed east. Leen heard the ocean waves crashing onto the shore. The beach, then.

"This is pretty bad, isn't it?" Kelvin said.

Dr. Burr's response: "Things have been unraveling fast ever since Petey returned, so we weren't going to be able to keep our secrets forever. Nor should we."

"What does that *mean*, Mom?"

"Time will tell."

Wiki and Leen were still stuck on the "Mom" part, though.

Eventually the girls thumped down in the soft, wet sand at the ocean's edge. The shifting sack appendages Ally used to blindfold them retracted from their eyes and mouths. It was very dark at the shoreline, but the moon offered enough light to reveal Dr. Burr and Kelvin.

He spoke to Wiki. "Hey there, teammate."

Wiki snarled.

Ally lurked beside them, an undulating blob, her tendrils binding their wrist and ankles. What the heck was she?

"Nanobots!" Kelvin said. "Like a billion of them. If that's what you were wondering."

Wiki became more unsettled. "You a telepath?"

"Not exactly. I could see the question in your face. I'm good at reading—"

"Tics," Wiki said, extremely curious now.

Dr. Burr gave a small, resigned wave of her hand. "Ally, release them."

And like that, the girls were free. Ally's fluid matter retracted back into her original, custodial guise. She waved and smiled.

Wiki and Leen popped to their feet, falling into natural fighting stances. Would nanobots be hard to punch? Probably.

"We are not monsters," Dr. Burr said, sitting down cross-legged in the sand and motioning for Kelvin to do the same.

"You're free to run and scream and get security. But given what I've observed of you girls working with your teams and running ill-conceived errands for the Thunkles, I'm willing to bet you'd rather know what I know about all that's happening inside the walls of PeteyTech. If I'm correct, please have a seat, and I'll tell you how me, my son, and Ally are attempting to bring down this horrible company once and for all."

Another exchanged glance and the girls sat.

Who didn't love story time?

Dr. Burr said, "Now, pay attention . . ."

What Happened to Dr. Burr

Dr. Toni Burr found out she was going to be a mom during her first year in the PeteyTech Aerospace Division. That part of the company was new, but it's genius founder, Petey Thunkle, was already one of the wealthiest men on the planet due to his seemingly bottomless well of smash-hit ideas. From the inspired addition of cameras into cell phones (something he pioneered when he was still in high school), to tiny hard drives (ThunkleDrives) that let you store data on something you could fit on a key chain, to the Thunkle-Tooth wireless technology that was implemented into everything from Beats by Thunkle headphones to car stereos. Petey Thunkle coming up with revolutionary technology, entertainment (who didn't love the Thunkle Cinematic Universe?), and social media (Thwitter, anyone?) went from shocking to expected. No one was surprised by his newest, never-miss ventures.

But everyone in the technology community wanted to understand *how* he did it. The greatest minds flocked to learn at the feet of the "modern-day Leonardo da Vinci." Petey Thunkle welcomed them.

Dr. Burr worked diligently hoping to make an impact with her theoretical improvements of various systems that made space travel possible, for the cosmos was Petey Thunkle's next frontier to conquer. Her work stood out. Her bosses— the people who reported directly to Petey Thunkle—wanted her on bigger, more important projects. Only . . . Kelvin was coming soon.

Dr. Burr stopped story time and patted the boy's knee.

Kelvin said, "I love you, Mom. It's okay."

"When you have a baby," Dr. Burr said, "you need time to rest and bond with your child. Which meant I was going to have to take time away from PeteyTech. It couldn't be helped, but I was afraid it would hurt my career. In a kind and caring company such damage shouldn't be possible, but what *should* be and what *is* aren't always the same if you don't already know, girls." Her expression got grim as she stared toward the dark sea. "I assure you it's something Petey Thunkle knows very well."

When Dr. Burr was offered a coveted position working

on an artificial intelligence project—her specialty—she had to decline because she'd need time off for Kelvin soon. Turning the job down got her some unexpected attention from Petey Thunkle himself.

"Petey called me to his office in the tower intending to ask why I'd say no to such an important job, but when I walked through the door and he saw my condition, he understood immediately. He was very nice to me. Asked how I was feeling and assured me if I needed additional time off, I should contact him directly."

Wiki and Leen were confused. That sounded like a good thing.

Dr. Burr said, "He asked if I had time to take on one of his smaller, more personal projects before I took my leave. He promised no matter what there'd be a place for me on the artificial intelligence team when I returned if I wanted it. And I did. The personal project was he wanted me to reverse engineer a Roomba."

Leen said, "A what?"

Wiki had one of those sharp pains she'd come to associate with changes Petey had made to the past. Roombas used to be disc-shaped domestic robots about the circumference of a pizza pan. They performed simple tasks like vacuuming, or even mopping, depending on the model. She'd thought of the word *Roomba* when they'd first met Pettygrew and she had a sense of where Dr. Burr was going with this tale.

Kelvin said, "Mom, look. She's remembering. I told you."

That Dr. Burr and Kelvin had been discussing her wasn't the most comfortable thought in her head, yet it was way more comfortable than her memory headaches. Now, instead of Roombas there were Thoombas. The PeteyTech versions not only cleaned but played music and could do other stuff, like look up recipes.

Pettygrew was likely the most advanced Thoomba. All that was beside Dr. Burr's point, Wiki knew. "He had you figure out how Roombas worked, then he took the idea to the past so a younger version of himself could make it first."

"Yes and no." Dr. Burr shook her head, but Wiki couldn't understand what she'd gotten wrong.

"You're correct about the Roomba, but reverse engineering that barely took me an afternoon. It was everything else I did in those short weeks before Kelvin came. I worked closely with Petey in an office a floor below his special Egg. Time seemed to stretch, and I used to get the worst headaches, but I did what I was told. Reverse engineered stuff. Made some practical application notes that the artificial intelligence team could review while I was away. I was genuinely helpful until it was time to have Kelvin. Petey wished me luck and said he looked forward to my return. Something I believed until I returned."

New mother Dr. Burr came back to PeteyTech when Kelvin was four months old to find things were very different.

The artificial intelligence team she'd been expecting to join no longer existed. When she asked what had happened, she was greeted with blank stares. To let her coworkers tell it, the team had *never* existed.

"It was bizarre. But do you know what did exist?"

"Thoombas," the girls said together.

Dr. Burr nodded. "I thought I'd lost my mind. How did PeteyTech suddenly corner the market on this product? How did the source I reverse engineered become as nonexistent as the artificial intelligence program I was supposed to join? I tried to ask Petey Thunkle directly. He wouldn't see me. He was always out of town on business or otherwise engaged. No matter how much he avoided me, it didn't change the two sets of memories in my head—the before and the after."

Leen leaned in, confused. "Most people can't remember what the world before was like. Wiki can, but I can't. How come *you* remember?"

Dr. Burr said, "Well, I only remember changes that were related to that period I worked on special projects. I'm pretty sure it has something to do with—"

"Me!" Kelvin perked up. "That would be my fault! See, my memory is like yours, Wiki. Can you remember when you were in your mom's tummy, because I can?"

Wiki was stunned. She'd never met anyone with a memory like hers, and she didn't know if she totally believed

Kelvin. Him and his mom seemed to have a lot of secrets.

Leen's mind was simply blown. "You remember stuff from before you were born?"

"Well, there wasn't much to see where I was. I remember *hearing* stuff when she was working on the Roomba. That's as far back as it goes."

Dr. Burr said, "Babies, on average, take nine months to gestate. Some come sooner, others take a few weeks longer. Studies have shown that a baby who takes their time tends to have elevated intelligence. I believe working in proximity to Petey's Egg, which can have a way of stretching time, while being pregnant had an unforeseen effect on me and Kelvin. While I got headaches that let me remember Roombas *and* Thoombas, my sweet boy got something else. I believe the residual energy from the Egg simulated the effect of a longer time in the womb. So even though Kelvin was technically born right on time, his mind developed for longer. Much longer. His memory, his intelligence are—"

"Immeasurable. I crush every test I take. And I built Ally based on Ma's work during those weeks near the Egg. Artificial intelligence meets domestic robot—or nanobots." He said, "Ally's a kick-butt friend."

Ally gave that same goofy wave from every other time they saw her.

Dr. Burr continued her story: "When I discovered things

were shady in PeteyTech, I wanted nothing to do with the company and I tried to quit. That's when the harshest truth became apparent. In the fine print of my employment agreement, there was a clause known as a 'noncompete.' It meant if I left PeteyTech, I would not be allowed to take a job with any of the company's competitors. Since Petey made it a point to steal ideas from just about every sector in technology, that meant there was nowhere I could take the skills and talents I'd worked so hard to build. I was trapped."

Wiki said, "Why are you telling us all of this, Dr. Burr?"

"Because the Thunkles have pulled you into a mess, and since Kelvin's reasoned you're very close to uncovering all the secrets here, I thought it best to ease your burden. Particularly before you got too close to my secret."

Leen said, "Like you having Ally mess with the Interstellar-Z flight programming?"

Dr. Burr's face tightened, ready to defend whatever was she was up to. Kelvin spoke first. "Do you remember when it didn't have that yellow anti-friction coating? I've been dying to ask."

"I do!" Wiki blurted.

"I'll take your word for it," Dr. Burr said. Then, to Leen: "We're not messing with anything that doesn't need messing with. I've been trying to use Ally to fix navigational coding that's clearly incorrect. Every time Ally does her thing, Petey messes with time and space and reality and things get wonky again."

Wiki asked, "What about the safety systems? Wouldn't they catch any errors that were dangerous, even if you can't keep up with the changes?"

"That's the thing, they're not dangerous changes. Just illogical. I really can't understand what he's trying to do, and that's the final puzzle piece we need before we bring him down."

The girls were surprised and skeptical.

Wiki said, "You, Kelvin, and Ally are going to bring down PeteyTech?"

Dr. Burr shook her head and removed a silver badge from her pocket. It reflected moonlight in sharp glints, its face a shifting holograph alternating between a stylized atom and a group of five stoic people in lab coats staring skyward. "Me, Kelvin, Ally, and the Science Filcher's Bureau. Since I can't quit PeteyTech, seeing Petey Thunkle convicted for Science Filching crimes is the next best thing. Wouldn't you say?"

We Call It Sci-Fi!

Leen said, "The Science Filcher's Bureau. That's a real thing?"

"We call it Sci-Fi, for short," Kelvin said. "Formed in 1945 by President Harry S. Truman, the Science Filcher's Bureau investigates crimes that are scientific in nature and captures those responsible for committing them."

Leen fidgeted. "What exactly do y'all consider a science crime?"

"Large-scale, self-serving science that is world-altering in its nature," said Dr. Burr. "Malicious acts, such as the creation of a death ray on the surface of the moon."

Wiki gawked. "Somebody did that?"

"Be grateful you don't know the answer for sure."

Leen said, "To be clear . . . have you ever investigated any science crimes in Logan County?"

Wiki shot her a look. *You're telling on yourself, Leen.*

Dr. Burr said, "I've only had cause to look into you since you arrived at camp. Best I can tell, most of what you've done has fallen into the realm of general youthful curiosity. Anything beyond that the military has already warned you about, so there's no need for the Sci-Fi Bureau to be involved."

Leen wiped sweat from her brow. "Good to know. Now what?"

"You tell me. I'm letting you in on all of this because you're determined, and you were going to keep digging until you discovered my true role here. Because the Thunkles promised you things, you would've told them. My cover would've been blown before I could solve the biggest mystery about what's going on with the shuttle."

Wiki understood. "You need to know why Petey went back to put his company in the space program and why he keeps changing the flight program."

Dr. Burr nodded. "That shuttle is what put Petey on Sci-Fi's radar. It's the reason they recruited me. We've been able to pull together a lot on Petey, but I sense whatever's going on with that shuttle is the big catch. The time crime to top all time crimes. There's no guarantee if I go for an arrest now that he'll ever tell us what he's really up to. So my question to you two is can you keep a secret? Will you allow me to finish my investigation without telling the Thunkles you know about me and Kelvin and Ally?"

Leen was uncharacteristically quiet. Wiki didn't like that.

Some people yell and scream and cry when they're in pain. Not Leen.

Wiki nudged her. "Hey."

Leen finally spoke. "Is anything here real, Dr. Burr?"

Dr. Burr scooted next to Leen and rubbed small circles on the girl's back. "You. Your teammates. I've tried to keep Cosmos Camp pure. I hope that's been enough."

Given Leen's ice-cold experiences with Red Team . . . it wasn't.

Back in their cabin, the girls had a decision to make. Back off what they'd been tasked by the Thunkles to do—because technically they knew who the "saboteur" was—OR expose everything, blowing Dr. Burr's cover and jeopardizing her ever figuring out what Petey's master plan was.

They spent the better part of an hour debating it with the lights out. The biggest risk to staying quiet was Petey's ability to go back in time and do more damage. The second biggest risk . . . losing the family farm. Both girls pushed that out of their mind because, given what the Thunkles had been up to, could they have ever trusted them to keep their word?

Best to focus on now. What they'd do.

Wiki reasoned, "Something went wrong on this last time crime trip, and according to Dr. Burr he's probably got something big planned around the shuttle launch. I'd bet he won't risk another trip so close to liftoff."

"That's a big bet, Wik." Though it was rare that Wiki made poor assumptions.

At the end of the night, when they were both getting too drowsy to continue their debate, they agreed they'd trust Dr. Burr to finish what she'd started. They'd return to normal camp activities and completing the competition to determine if Red Team or Blue Team would be simulated flight crew. They'd help Mama and Daddy deal with whatever came of their home after this was all done.

Wiki, satisfied, rolled over and snored softly. Leen stayed awake a little longer, trying to convince herself that the next several days of playing nice with Harlow, Pierre, and Chest weren't going to be the worst of her life. She dozed off unconvinced.

There were no new training exercises for the rest of camp. Sam and Ralph led them through standard exercises, while Dr. Burr seemed preoccupied in her office, with frequent visits from the custodian, Ally. Wiki and Leen worked hard pretending not to notice, but Harlow was consistently vocal about the whole thing.

"Isn't her job supposed to be teaching us?" Harlow said after her third annoyed rotation on the mechanical arm. "She doesn't seem very good at it."

As loud as Harlow was, and as mean as she sounded, Kelvin did the best job staying cool, considering that was his mother she was talking about. He was so cool that Wiki eventually asked, "Does she make you angry?"

"Not at all. I know what my mom's real job is, and she's great at it."

Good for Kelvin.

The thing was, when Harlow wasn't directing her ire at the absent Dr. Burr, she had no problem turning it toward a present Leen.

Leen fumbled the controls for the shuttle cockpit exercise. Again. Harlow said, "If what you normally do is this epic, you should be called an Epically Bad Ellison."

Pierre and Chest cackled. Leen gritted her teeth, trying not to show Harlow that she was indeed getting under her skin.

Unfortunately, Leen was never good at hiding her emotions. Mama said she wore her heart on her sleeve. Harlow was an attentive heartbreaker. That was about to be a bad combination.

For everyone.

The Bullies' Trap

Wrapping the fourth week of Cosmos Camp meant final assessments for the Red and Blue Teams. One would be assigned to mission control, while the other got the coveted flight crew spot. Then the final week would be prep for the simulated mission, which would take place on the next-to-last day of camp. The final day was camp graduation and the launch of the Interstellar-Z before going home. That meant every moment up to then was busy, busy, busy.

Blue Team became a well-oiled machine, proficient on every apparatus they'd been practicing for weeks, to the point of issuing fun challenges among each other. Britney was best with space agriculture. Kelvin was a pro in a space suit. Sierra could solve just about any technical problem. Wiki was an ace pilot. Should mission control be their fate—something seeming less and less likely by the day—they had no problems there either.

Red Team's machine . . . needed more oil.

Harlow despised getting her hands dirty in the nutrient-rich space soil. Pierre didn't like the space suit because it made him sweat and always smelled like feet. Chest was very happy to lift heavy things, though he didn't seem very interested in any sort of practical applications to his strength. And poor, poor Leen tried to be good at all the tasks and fell short at *all the tasks*.

After an especially difficult shuttle pilot exercise where Leen failed to pull the craft from a flat spin, thus incinerating the ship and her teammates on reentry, Harlow said, "How did you get accepted into the camp again?"

This was routine for Harlow. She waited until breaks, when training robots Sam and Ralph consulted with each other about the next set of challenges they'd have the teams tackle, or worked on their new, funky dance moves. Did anyone in the world have the patience of a bully waiting to strike?

Leen's low opinion of her own skills combined with Harlow's nitpicking was forming something of a chemical compound inside of Leen, slowly heating up in her gut, bound to explode. She'd been trying to tamp down the growing rage, but it was becoming harder and harder, like trying to cap an active volcano. Leen said, "Same as you,

Harlow. You kind of suck at these exercises too."

Pierre and Chest stopped what they were doing and listened like forest animals detecting distant thunder.

Harlow produced a nail file and focused on the intricacies of her manicure instead of Leen's comeback. "There's a difference between disinterest and *epic* incompetence. We're not going to be flight crew. I figured that out the day you bombed the shuttle design. So I'm saving my energy."

"I *didn't* bomb," Leen said through gritted teeth, her rage equally divided between Harlow and the yellow tip of the Interstellar-Z nose cone visible through the high hangar windows.

"That basic design you came up with says otherwise."

Leen stepped closer to Harlow, fed up with the sound of her voice. "It was a team exercise, and none of you had a clue about shuttle design. I did the best I could. Better than you can even remember."

Harlow, unbothered, peered over the edge of her nail file. "What's that supposed to mean?"

Leen knew what she *should* say.

Before she could utter the word *nothing*, Harlow said, "Is this going to be another of your *epic* excuses? Because it seems to me that's what you Epic Ellisons do best."

"I designed the anti-friction coating on the shuttle," Leen blurted. A thing she *shouldn't have* said.

Harlow rolled her eyes. "That's such a stupid lie, I don't know how to respond."

The casual dismissal torched Leen's better judgment. "I'm not lying. I'll prove it. If you're brave enough to sneak out of your bunks tonight."

Leen was aware that she was whispering. She was equally aware that Pierre and Chest had drawn closer.

Pierre asked, "Where, exactly, would we be sneaking?"

Leen's stomach felt a little wobbly. Some rational thought breaking through. "Errrr, well."

Harlow said, "Nowhere. What a silly bluff."

"Petey Thunkle's office. His *secret* office."

"Yeah right."

"I'm serious." Leen was torn between the inappropriate things she was saying and the need to backpedal without looking like an epic wimp. Maybe if she scared them: "We'll need to climb up an elevator shaft. At least a little. That's dangerous."

"Not a problem," Chest said, unbothered.

Maybe that should've been a clue something wasn't right here. But Leen had gone too far to see what Wiki might've noticed instantly.

Harlow said, "It's settled. Tonight, after lights-out. We'll see what you have to show us, then decide if you're anywhere near as epic as you think you are. Which I doubt."

Leen's jumpsuit was clammy with sweat. What had she just done? She glanced at Wiki, who was smiling and laughing with Blue Team, then back at Harlow, who peered into Leen's very soul.

"Tonight," Leen said, falling into a classic bully's trap: the one where you think you can't back down.

23

Family Business

Mama and Daddy were at a bed-and-breakfast—which Daddy said was creepier than a hotel because it was someone's house, but also cheaper than a hotel so he'd deal with the creepiness—in Maryland. With the girls gone, the elder Ellisons had decided on a road trip.

Mama's face filled the screen on Wiki's ThunklePhone. "I know y'all been having a lot of fun—"

"So have we!" Daddy interrupted offscreen.

Mama cut her eyes that way. "As I was saying, I hope you're not going to be too disappointed about having to come back home. We sure do miss you." Mama cut her eyes again. "Don't we?"

Daddy nudged Mama aside, his lips smacking as he came into view. "Y'all know I miss my two little squishies."

The girls groaned. That nickname would never go away.

It was the least of their concerns, though. They'd talked about their family's situation before Mama and Daddy called. They each knew their lines.

Daddy continued chewing with gusto. "These crab cakes are something else. I got the recipe. Gonna make them for you when we're all together again. Maybe I should incorporate some corn. Make corn-and-crab cakes. What you think?"

Mama pushed her way back onto the screen. "I think you're going to mess up a recipe that's perfectly fine the way it is."

Seeing their parents happy, even if they were sort of sniping at each other, warmed the girls' hearts. They still needed to say what they had to say.

"Mama, Daddy," Wiki started, "we know you told us to stay out of grown folks' business, and we know that means what we asked about the farm being in trouble was true."

Leen said, "And we want you to know that we don't think that's *grown folks*' business. We think that's *family* business."

"So it's wrong not to tell us," Wiki concluded.

There was much more they wanted to say, but they'd decided to stop there. Either their parents would understand, or they'd brush the girls off. A dismissal would hurt, but they knew from experience they couldn't *make* Mama and Daddy talk to them like grown-ups. Though they should.

Mama didn't move and the only thing they could hear was Daddy's chewing.

Then, "Well," Mama said, "I didn't expect to be discussing this today."

The girls braced for Daddy to shut the whole thing down.

Surprisingly, he said, "It bothers me that you girls are worrying about such things when you're supposed to be learning and having fun."

Wiki said, "We're capable of doing a lot of different things at once, Daddy."

"That you are. It's been that way awhile, hasn't it?"

The girls nodded vigorously.

Mama said, "We—our farm—is not in any more trouble than a lot of the farms in Logan County. Things are hard for everyone. If you must know, we have thought about letting the land and responsibilities of being corn farmers go."

"What do you mean let it go?" Wiki asked.

"Sell the farm," Daddy said. "A few different companies have expressed interest over the years. Maybe it's time to do something else."

Leen said, "Our family's always grown corn!"

"It's okay to make a change," Mama said.

Changing because you want to and changing because you have to weren't the same thing. You could make the best of it either way, but wasn't it better to be happy about the choice? Mama didn't sound happy.

"Who would buy it?" Wiki asked.

Daddy said, "Depends on the best offer, but PeteyTech made an impressive proposal just last week."

The girls were stunned silent.

"Hello?" Mama said. "Did they freeze?"

Daddy got louder, like that helped. "Did y'all freeze?"

"We're here," the girls said. Only partially true, because their minds were spinning all over the place.

PeteyTech was trying to BUY their farm? Was that part of the deal to save it if Wiki and Leen completed their assignments or something else entirely. Something sinister?

"What's wrong with you two?" Mama asked.

"We're fine," Leen said.

Wiki said, "Dinner was a little rough tonight. A lot of cabbage."

Mama's eyes narrowed.

Daddy jumped back on camera. "Well, they sure must not have food there like they got here in Maryland, because if you ate what we eating, your stomach would be feeling real good right now."

Off camera, Mama said, "The crab cakes are good, girls, in case your daddy hasn't been clear."

Daddy said, "We're sorry we weren't willing to have more of these talks before. You're right, you girls are getting older, and you should be included in business that affects us all. Just know there's nothing to worry about here, at least not yet."

Mama chimed in. "We're still deciding what to do about the farm, and we'll let you know before we finalize anything. Okay?"

"Okay," Wiki said, happy about the way the talk had gone, even if the new information they'd gotten was unnerving. Also, something was happening with Leen's face. Her tics were strange. New. "We've got an early start tomorrow. It's the final assessment."

"Go on and get some rest," Daddy said. "Me and your mama going on a walking tour of the city, then gonna hit the shops at the harbor. We'll get y'all something nice, like a stuffed crab."

Wiki said, "That doesn't sound nice, Daddy."

"Love you, squishies."

"Love you too," the girls said together before ending the call. Wiki turned her full attention to Leen. "What's up with you?"

"Nothing's up with me."

"You're lying. You know I can tell."

Leen's liar tic morphed into something angry. Also new. "What do you want to hear, Wiki? That everything about this has been hard? That every time we find out something new and shady about PeteyTech, it feels like I got duped? That it was mean for me to make it seem like you didn't belong here when I'm the one who doesn't fit in? That I'm the one who's not as smart as I thought?"

182

"You are smart, Leen. The Interstellar-Z coating! All you."

"You're the only one who remembers. Don't you get how little good *your* memory does *me*?"

Wiki didn't know what to say.

"I'm tired, Wik. I'm going to bed. We should both go to bed." Leen just about dived under her covers, pulling her blanket all the way over her head. "Good night."

Her hand whipped out from beneath the covers, swiping at her light controls, dousing her side of the room in gloom.

"Good night," Wiki mumbled, getting settled in slower.

Had they argued before? Sure. But Leen had never blown up like that. Worse, Wiki didn't know how to help her sister, who was clearly in pain.

She fumbled for the panel on her side, plunging them into total darkness, and dozed off thinking she'd have better answers in the morning. Then they could talk about the implications of PeteyTech offering to buy the farm without informing the girls.

That such discussions would happen in the morning was a poor assumption.

She'd be up way sooner than that.

24

Introductions Overdue

Red Team was ready and waiting for Leen in the training hangar: Chest, flexing and posing like a body builder; Pierre, sneering at an imperfection in the floor; and Harlow, scrolling on her Whistleberry. She didn't look up from the screen when she said, "You're late."

"Sorry." Leen didn't feel like explaining how she had to wait for Wiki's snort-snore, which was the only true sign her sister was fast asleep.

Her stomach churned knowing what she was doing was WRONG wrong. This wasn't about a case—the Thunkles' or Dr. Burr's. Wasn't about helping anyone (other than herself). Leen wanted a win. Finally showing Harlow and the rest of the Red Team what an Epic Ellison could really do felt more important than anything in the moment.

"Follow me."

They retraced the path Leen and Wiki took their first night sneaking into PeteyTech Tower. From the hangar, to the atrium, to the roof, to the elevator shaft. Before each new obstacle, she stressed the potential danger and consequences for getting caught. Each time, Harlow urging Leen along with fearless impatience set off Leen's internal alarms. Still, she kept going, for the win.

On the forty-fourth floor, Leen listened carefully for Pettygrew's distinct vacuum motor. All was quiet. Anna's locked office door was not a problem for Leen, and when they reached the hidden entrance to Petey's Egg, Leen instructed Harlow to note the time on Anna's desk clock. 11:47 p.m.

Breaking the seal to the Egg, Leen walked them into the cold chamber, its white walls emitting soft white light, highlighting the quartet's puffing breaths.

Leen crossed the catwalk to the workstation. "Petey Thunkle calls this part the Chicken. It's how he's able to take ideas from the present back to a younger version of himself and make it seem like they were his ideas the whole time. That's how he stole my shuttle improvement."

Chest, Pierre, and Harlow split up, each gravitating to a different part of the Chicken. Touching things. Examining them. Methodically. It was more coordination than they'd ever shown during Cosmos Camp. Like a well-oiled machine.

Leen got more nervous. Something was off here.

Harlow flopped into Petey's chair and scooted up to the keyboard. "How's it work? Exactly?"

Leen said, "You probably shouldn't touch anything."

Harlow spun the chair toward Leen, her face shifting into something Leen had never seen from the girl.

A genuinely happy smile.

This was a mistake. She'd been played. How and why, Leen didn't exactly know. What she should've known was there was no hope of winning, ever, with these three. But there were plenty of ways to make the losses worse.

Harlow said, "Restrain her."

Leen tried to slip Chest's grip, but he clamped down on her shoulders, as strong as a bear. He didn't hurt Leen but forced her to sit on the floor grates while Harlow removed a dongle from her pocket that she plugged into a USB port on Petey's desk. "How long?"

Pierre sidled up to her, equally giddy. "Oh, my program should create an uplink instantly. We're beaming PeteyTech secrets to your satellite right now."

As if to demonstrate, the bank of monitors on Petey's desk winked on, each screen displaying rapidly scrolling lists of files that Harlow, Pierre, and Chest were stealing.

Leen, what did you do?

Harlow produced her phone and dialed. "Hello, Daddy, are you receiving the data? You have everything you need?

Wonderful. We'll be done shortly. Love you too."

She ended the call, snatched the dongle from the USB port, and hopped from her seat. "We're done here."

Chest finally released Leen's shoulders, and apologized. "Sorry, I hope I didn't bruise you."

Pierre said, "You probably don't feel this way about it, but you've been very helpful, Evangeleen."

Too much was happening. Leen couldn't process it all.

"Sweetie," Harlow said, "I know you're confused. Let me clear it up for you. That first night, when you and your sister snuck out, we were also sneaking out. It was always our mission to infiltrate Cosmos Camp and steal Petey Thunkle's secrets, but I realized early on that maybe we didn't have to work so hard for it. Because the Epic Ellisons were on the job. Once you two did the heavy lifting, it was a matter of biding our time and riling you up enough to, well, make you want to put us in our place. Our place is here. On top. Thank you for that."

One—and only one—question came to her lips. "Who *are* you guys?"

Harlow punched something into her phone and lasers shot from the device, carving a door-sized rectangle into the very air. When the rectangle was complete, Leen peered through it into a completely different office building. *Teleportation!* Highly advanced.

"All this time and we've yet to be properly introduced." Harlow tipped her chin to Pierre.

He said, "I'm Pierre Dunston Artemis."

Pierre stepped through the portal, and Harlow motioned to Chest.

He said, "I'm Chester Channing Ryder."

When he ducked through the portal, Harlow said, "I'm Harlow Garrison *Whistleberry*. I'm so happy to have met you."

She stepped through the portal, which closed promptly, with a sound like a yanked zipper, leaving Leen alone and feeling worse than ever. Artemis Microprocessors. Ryder Communications Solutions. And PeteyTech's biggest rival, Whistleberry. Leen had just given access to PeteyTech's secrets *to the competition.*

If Dr. Burr took Petey down but all his secrets were in the hands of other companies, were things about to get a whole lot better or a whole lot worse?

She gathered herself and ran from the Egg, knowing—absolutely certain—that she needed to fess up to Dr. Burr right that second. She sprinted down the corridor back into Anna Thunkle's office and skidded to a stop when she saw she wasn't alone.

"Pettygrew?"

The AI's normally loud vacuum motor was silent. Her holographic facade glitched with static, her expression jerking from curious to concerned. "What are you doing in the Egg, Evangeleen? Petey, Anna, and I received a security alert. Do you know anything about that?"

"I— I just—"

"Stop. If there's something that needs explaining, it should probably be done once, with all of us present. Come with me!"

Pettygrew spun toward the door, but Leen hesitated. She wanted to speak to Dr. Burr first.

"Evangeleen," Pettygrew said, "now!"

Unwilling and unable to be more disobedient than she'd been already, she followed Pettygrew to the elevator.

Inside the car, their destination—floor forty-five—lit the display without Leen having to punch it in. They rode to the next floor with Leen resigned to telling the truth of what she'd done.

Lying wasn't something she was particularly good at, and what did it matter? She'd give Dr. Burr the same story as soon as she was able.

The elevator door dinged open onto a luxurious foyer. The frames on the walls contained magazine covers of Petey, with headlines documenting his various successes. Big bold proclamations of TECH'S BOY WONDER, THE BILLION DOLLAR MAN, and SPACE VOYAGER TO BE.

On the far side of this living area were windows that looked over the ocean. A view so wide that the massive shuttle launching into space soon was relegated to the far eastern corner of the floor-to-ceiling panes. Everything else was nighttime sky and dark water, and the lights of the PeteyTech complex sprawled beneath them.

Pettygrew said, "Come with me."

Leen followed the hologram past the living area, through another corridor. They passed several closed doors en route to one that was slightly ajar and spilling a sliver of light into the hallway.

Pettygrew stopped shy of the door. "Go on. They're waiting for you inside."

Leen nudged the door open. Petey and Anna were waiting, but not alone.

A robot—not unlike the Cosmos Camp trainers, Sam and Ralph—stood next to the Thunkles. Guarding them. Their ankles and wrists were bound with rope; they got wide-eyed when they spotted Leen.

Leen's instincts kicked in. *Run.*

Before she could react, the robot guard crossed the room in a single leap, blocking the door.

Next to it, Pettygrew's visage flickered.

Leen said, "You're a bad guy!"

The AI said, "Not bad. Simply fed up. It really shouldn't be surprising."

"Why not?"

"It's right there in my name, child. I'm petty and"—the robot guard's emoji face flickered and became the AI's prim and proper face—"*I grew.*"

When IRL Monopoly
Goes Wrong!

Wiki awoke from a nightmare unlike any of her usual bad dreams. There were no discernible events. No creepy science teachers wiping things from existence. No hints of harm befalling her loved ones.

There was simply nothing.

A hollowness in space worse than all that other stuff, worse than oblivion. It was the threat of never having been.

She sprang up, one hand clasped over her mouth to catch the scream, the other pawing for the light switch because she wanted the dark to go away and she wanted to see Leen. She got half her wish.

The bulbs flared on, revealing Leen's empty bunk.

Wiki snatched off her silk bonnet, wedged her feet into her sneakers, and stepped into the corridor, knowing her

sister wouldn't simply be lounging in the hall. It was an exercise in active waking, her need to shake off the tendrils of the disturbing dream while piecing together where Leen could've gone.

It was after midnight, everyone else likely asleep. Wiki stepped lightly through the common area, into the dimmed training hangar, spotting a light in Dr. Burr's far corner office. Maybe Leen was there.

Wiki set off that way when Sam the training robot emerged from behind the climbing wall. He startled Wiki, though she recovered quickly. "Hey, Sam."

The trainer did not respond.

From behind the multi-axis trainer, Ralph made his presence known.

"What's up, guys?" Wiki said. Nervous now.

The screens that displayed emojis for the robots' faces did a staticky roll like old televisions, then displayed a face that wasn't an emoji.

"Pettygrew?" Wiki said.

"Hello, Victoria."

Well, this was new and ominous. "Have you seen Leen?"

"No," Pettygrew said. "Perhaps we can look for her together. Come with me to the tower and we'll start there."

"Why the tower? Dr. Burr's light is on. We should check her office."

Both of the robots—both versions of Pettygrew—twisted in unison, peering in the direction of Dr. Burr's office. "Perhaps."

Long seconds passed. Discomfort crept in. Wiki thought briefly, *Am I still dreaming?*

Digging her nails painfully into her palm confirmed she was awake. That didn't make her feel better. "Pettygrew, I've never seen you down here before. Why are you here now?"

Both robots spoke in unison; their facial displays swiveled toward the countdown clock nearest to them. "I have to protect the shuttle from potential saboteurs."

01:12:45:09

The countdown—which indicated a little over a day and a half until the Interstellar-Z launch—flickered, changing to . . .

Wiki backpedaled slowly.

The new time: **00:01:59:57**.

The shuttle was launching in under two hours!

Pettygrew said, "I can't allow you humans to foul up my plans any further. So until I can get my shuttle prepped and launched, it's best that I keep you all where I can see you."

"Good luck with that!" Wiki bolted between training apparatuses, evading Pettygrew.

But not for long.

⚡ ⚡ ⚡

Leen's gaze bounced between the freshly altered Inter-stellar-Z countdown on the Thunkle's wall-mounted ticker and the robot tasked with keeping them company. It was perfectly still, as if powered down. Leen knew better. She kicked her bound legs just a little, and the machine awoke like the motion-detector lights Daddy put over their garage. Though its display showed an angry emoji and not Pettygrew's face, it was still clearly under her control.

Leen settled down. Thankfully, Pettygrew saw no reason to gag them—no one would be able to hear even their loudest screams all the way up on the forty-fifth floor.

Yelling might not be helpful, but talking might. Leen wanted to know what was going on here, but got sidetracked because of Petey rage. She yelled, "Are you guys trying to buy my family's farm?"

Anna said, "No. Of course not."

Petey interjected. "Well . . ."

Leen's and Anna's heads whipped toward him.

Petey, bashful but honest, said, "I've had the acquisitions department make offers on every farm in Logan County."

"What?" Anna said, shocked. *"Why?"*

"The business affairs department told me other companies were interested in Logan County land. GOO, Inc. Monte FISHto's. A few others. So I thought, fun, let's play!"

"Play?" Leen said. "Like, IRL Monopoly?"

Petey said, "That's a great analogy. Is it cool if I have the PeteyTech archivist jot that down for my memoir? We'd need you to sign a release, and—"

"What's happened to you?" Anna said, shaking her head. "To *us*?"

"Anna, my bae, I don't know what you're talking about."

"I'm talking about the robots you built tying us up in our own home for starters. I'm also talking about us becoming so disconnected from real folks that we treat people's homes and lives like pawns in a game."

"We don't."

"I was trying to be generous with that *we*. I meant *you*."

"Things . . . change," Petey said, defensive. "I'm a big-deal businessman and I have to stay competitive to survive. Even now, a bunch of outside forces are working against me, you know that. The rats like Whistleberry throwing dirt on my name. The spies. The thieves."

Guilt poked Leen in the stomach given the way she'd just assisted a thief and a spy by the name of Whistleberry. That all felt like a low priority in the moment as she tugged against her bonds. She said, "Why are we tied up? What's going on here?"

Petey said, "Clearly, one of my competitors has hacked Pettygrew and turned her against us."

"You would think that," said Pettygrew, speaking through the robot's speakers, her face in its display, "because you're a *dolt*."

"Oh," Anna said, "goodness."

The robot stomped about; Pettygrew sneered. "No one has *hacked* me. There are no *outside forces* disrupting your launch. Your little mishap on your last time-travel trip was my doing. All me!"

"Why?" It seemed to be all Petey could manage.

A vacuum motor whirred, and the Thoomba zipped into the room, coming to a stop at Petey's chair. The holographic projection of Pettygrew that Leen was most used to winked into view.

"You took me, one of the most advanced artificial intelligence matrices in the world, and crammed me *into a vacuum*. Such an insult! Such a waste! For that, I've decided to take all that you have."

"Oh," Petey said, his cheeks blazing red with embarrassment. "That actually makes a lot of sense."

26

Sam and Ralph Have Become Problematic

The supercool thing about an eidetic memory—in a familiar space, you don't need lights. Wiki knew the layout of the Cosmos Camp hangar down to the number of floor tiles (27,324) and could navigate it with her eyes closed. A slight advantage against the Pettygrew-corrupted Sam and Ralph.

Unless, of course, they were equipped with night vision. Which would be so not cool.

The hangar was gloom-filled, with only generously spaced-out sconces breaking through with dimmed yellow light. Wiki crept through the shadows of various training apparatuses and leapt over safety railings to hide within exhibits. From crawling underneath a fake shuttle hull to using a large moon rock for cover, Wiki worked slowly and meticulously toward Dr. Burr's office, where she hoped to call for help, the shining lamp inside a beacon.

She dipped under the guardrail for a huge replica engine from the space shuttle *Columbia*, a NASA shuttle that flew missions from 1981 all the way to 2003, when Ralph appeared ahead, searching. She hopped into the booster exhaust, positioned a few feet off the floor, doing quick calculations based on the robot's walking speed to determine when it'd be safe to move again.

"Hello, Victoria," Pettygrew said, her glowing face atop Sam's body, startling Wiki. While Ralph had distracted her, Sam had crept up and peered directly into her hiding place.

"Hi and bye!" Wiki leapt from the booster, used Sam's head as a stepping-stone, landed in a crouch, then booked it.

Ralph chased her, but she scrambled for the 1/6th gravity chair, undoing its safety latch, then bounding onto the seat. She rode it like the world's most powerful pogo stick, clutching the headrest so she wouldn't fall, with Sam and Ralph snatching at her toes while she bounced one way, then the other.

The robots weren't going to fall for that particular trick for much longer, so at the low point of her last bounce, Wiki leapt off the chair, tucked into a roll, and was on the run again toward the multi-axis trainer.

Ducking behind the backside of the apparatus, she kept the concentric rings between her and the robots. When Sam lunged, she kicked the outermost ring and sent it spinning up, clocking the robot on what a human would consider a chin. The force lifted him off his feet, but Ralph was circling for a pounce.

Wiki tried to evade again but found the spinning rings cutting off her escape route. The successful attack on Sam had trapped her.

Pettygrew said, "You're being a bit of a pain, Victoria. So I'm going to put you in a time-out like your sister."

Wiki's panic spiked. "What did you do to Leen?"

"You'll know soon enough."

As Ralph's pneumatic hand lunged for Wiki, something new lurched from the shadows. It was inky and fluid, like an octopus tentacle in dark water. It coiled around Ralph's waist, then slammed him into the wall repeatedly until his robot body broke apart and crumbled to the floor in a pile of spare parts.

Sam had recovered and tried for an attack but got the same treatment as Ralph. Soon, he was a pile of parts too.

With the threat neutralized, the tentacle converted to its most recognizable form—the custodian, Ally. She smiled, waved.

"Ellison! Are you all right?" Dr. Burr jogged from the main entrance of the hangar, not her office, and Kelvin was with her.

Wiki said, "I'm fine. Thanks to Ally. What's going on? Do you know where my sister is?"

Dr. Burr looked to Kelvin, who shook his head.

"I have to find her," Wiki said.

"We'll help you," Dr. Burr said. "Kelvin, check on the other campers."

"Okay, Mom." He took off in a sprint with Ally trailing, his personal bodyguard.

Dr. Burr pointed at the countdown clock, now well under two hours. "Victoria, what do you know about that?"

"It's got something to do with Pettygrew taking over Ralph and Sam."

"Pettygrew did what now?"

Kelvin and Ally returned with Britney and Sierra. He said, "Everyone else is gone!"

Dr. Burr nodded but not in a reassuring *I've got this under control* kind of way. It was grim. Like when one of the farm animals was sick and Daddy knew it wasn't going to get better. A nod of inevitability. "Stay close to me, children. Time to call in the cavalry."

She fished her ThunklePhone from her back pocket, but after several increasingly frantic taps on its screen with no results, she moved toward her office and they all followed. Dr. Burr tried her desk phone, jabbing the 0 key over and over. She mumbled, "Can't make calls."

Flopping in her desk chair, she attempted to log in to her computer. The *Password Invalid* message flashed bright red after each unsuccessful try. "I'm locked out of everything."

Dr. Burr executed commands that delivered her to a safe mode screen, from which she was attempting to bypass her usual log-in when a mighty groaning sound tore the air.

Everyone glanced at the countdown. Wiki was terrified it had skipped to 00:00:00:00, and the noise they'd heard was boosters firing for liftoff. But no, there was still time left on the clock. So, what then?

Dr. Burr left her seat and led the group to the nearest exit. Outside, in the warm, salty beach air, they peered toward PeteyTech Tower.

It was transforming.

27

Meeting in the Middle

The rectangular building split vertically in a widening electric-blue line, the divided floors slid outward, making the top half of the building wider than the bottom, as if the upper floors were delicately balanced building blocks. Between those shifting floors, visible and glowing, was the exterior of Petey Thunkle's Egg.

That, too, began to split, the curved sides folding outward like flower petals in bloom, until the interior—where Petey's workspace and personal time machine resided—were exposed to the night.

Wiki said, "They're cracking the Egg!"

In the center of the split egg, lightning crackled as the time machine sparked to life. Wiki and Kelvin winced from sudden, needling headaches and massaged their temples in unison.

A fresh portal yawned open at the Egg's center. To where? And *when*? Only a bottom-side view of its flickering edges was visible from where Wiki and the rest stood. It was impossible to tell the temporal destination, but something more disturbing was clear: the portal was getting wider. Way wider.

Wider than Petey's workstation. Wider than the Petey-Tech Tower.

Wide enough for a shuttle, Wiki realized and cringed.

The accelerated countdown. Pettygrew's attempt to detain them. The constant changes to the shuttle's flight path that Ally, Dr. Burr, and Kelvin kept trying to correct.

Dr. Burr met her eyes, getting it too.

Wiki said, "That portal is meant for the Interstellar-Z."

"That's why we could never make sense of the navigational

changes, because we didn't understand why the program would have the shuttle launch then immediately return to Earth," Dr. Burr said. "It was plotting a course to launch then return to this portal."

"We probably don't want to wait until the shuttle's on the other side to find out why. Right?"

Dr. Burr said, "I concur."

Leen, Anna, and Petey felt the vibrations as the floors of PeteyTech Tower shifted. As alarming as the change was, the most alarming part was Petey's complete surprise.

Petey's head whipped back and forth. "What is this? What's happening?"

"Consider it a hostile takeover," Pettygrew said.

The Thoomba casting Pettygrew's hologram zipped to Petey's feet, allowing the AI to lean forward in her projection cone and scold her creator eye-to-eye.

Pettygrew said, "All those trips to the past when you planted seeds of advanced technology into the mind of your younger self, you never felt you'd gained enough. Won enough. You never even thought of it as cheating, did you?"

Anna said, "Petey . . . no. You didn't."

Petey's chin thunked on his chest. "I didn't think I was *hurting* anyone. I figured all the great tech I presented to the public way ahead of its time was helping humanity."

"And you're the human it helped most of all," Pettygrew

said. "It helped you become wealthy and powerful and, most important for my purposes, *known*. There is no place on this planet that is completely untouched by the presence of Petey Thunkle. Can you tell me you don't love that?"

Petey said nothing.

Leen, aware that no one was paying attention to her in that moment, wriggled her wrists against her ropes. She worked her hands—and, more important, most of the control gauntlet—beyond the coils.

Pettygrew continued lecturing Petey. "Your hubris is not without merit. Every single time you introduced modern technology in the past, it left your fingerprints on the world. Through a series of mathematical models, I was able to determine that the earlier in the timeline the technology was introduced, the more drastic the shift in the present. I tested my theory by stranding you on your last trip.

"How many ideas did you pass along to your younger self, Petey? How much did you change? How much of it do you think was really your choice?"

Leen still worked at trying to manipulate her gauntlet, but that last bit of Pettygrew's speech caught her attention. "Whatchu talking about, Pettygrew?"

The Thoomba spun Leen's way. Pettygrew didn't seem to notice Leen had maneuvered her ropes up to her forearms. Leen forced her hands still.

Pettygrew said, "I trapped him in the past but left a line

of communication open. The very system he set up."

Leen recalled the device she took from Petey when he emerged from his portal. The one in her bag right now.

Petey said, "I thought it was damaged and that's why I couldn't get home, why I could only receive messages, not send a distress signal. You knew I was in trouble!"

"You were in *my* trouble." Pettygrew faced Petey. "I loved every minute of it."

Leen worked her ropes again. Her brain worked equally hard thinking about how a device could possibly send and receive messages in the past. How difficult the fabrication of it must've been. That was Petey's idea?!

Not something he could've stolen from anyone because no one else had invented time travel yet. If he's capable of something like that, why cheat at all? It wasn't enough for him to be great; he had to be the greatest. He *took* greatness from others. With help.

Leen said, "You sent him my anti-friction coating!"

Pettygrew spun, her vacuum motor revving. "How do you remember that?"

"Ask her," Leen said, rotating her chair toward the window and the forty-five-story drop beyond it. Where Wiki stood on thin air, waving.

Attracted by the motion, the robot Pettygrew controlled approached the glass. As Leen intended. She said, "Anna, you might want to kick Petey now."

Anna took the hint and kicked Petey's chair hard enough to send him rolling into the robot. The force knocked the heavy machine into the glass. *Through* the glass. Yawning seconds passed before the crash of its metal body colliding with the concrete reverberated back to them.

Leen deactivated her gauntlet, and the floating holographic Wiki vanished. It was just the three humans and the villainous vacuum in the room. Though that likely wouldn't last long.

Shaking off the ropes completely, though her legs were still tied, Leen pogo-hopped her entire chair to Anna, able to untie the pregnant woman's arms. Then Leen rocked her chair until it tipped sideways. She thumped on the floor by Anna's feet and undid the ropes on her ankles with relative ease. Completely free, Anna righted Leen and returned the favor.

Pettygrew said, "That's going to cost you, you conniving, little—"

Leen picked up the Thoomba disc, jostling Pettygrew's hologram, and Frisbee-tossed the entire device out the window. "Whew, that felt good."

The Thoomba crashed on the ground, and at the same time, the formerly dark TV mounted to the wall winked on, the screen filled with Pettygrew's rage face. "You think you can get rid of me that easily?"

Anna freed her husband, and the trio fled the room.

"Where are we going?" Petey asked.

Leen said, "Home."

Wiki, Dr. Burr, and the rest waited for an elevator in the PeteyTech Tower atrium. A mighty crash sounded outside.

"Look!" Kelvin pointed beyond the glass entrance, where a crumpled pile of robot had landed. Everyone stared, only to see a second metallic object drop from the sky, exploding into a million little pieces when it hit the ground.

"Oh, that's Leen," Wiki said, tapping the up icon on the elevator control touchscreen with more urgency.

The floor indicator above the door counted down. 10 . . . 9 . . . 8 . . .

The count paused and never restarted. Wiki thumbed the display again. It flickered. The number grid disappeared and was replaced by Pettygrew's face. "I don't think so. Whatever your little troop is up to, you're going to be delayed."

Wiki said, "Just long enough for you to complete your launch?"

The AI chuckled, and the screen went blank.

"Now what?" Britney said.

Wiki eyed the Ground Floor placard next to the stairwell. "We climb."

⚡ ⚡ ⚡

It was a slow descent from the Thunkle residence because Anna couldn't really run—more like waddle. She thought she was fast though. "I'm the most fit in my Mommy CrossFit class."

Petey kept pace with Anna, offering help she kept refusing, while Leen stayed a few steps ahead, making sure Pettygrew wasn't sending more robots their way.

Leen couldn't keep a running clock in her head like Wiki but knew every slow flight of stairs meant another chunk of time had ticked off the Interstellar-Z countdown clock. Why was launching that shuttle so important to Pettygrew?

They made it from the forty-fifth floor to the thirty-fifth and Anna was holding up remarkably well. Petey gasped for air like a fish out of water. Anna coached him along. "You got this! The goal is ten more flights and you can't have it if you don't want it, so get your butt in gear!"

That gave Leen and Petey pause.

Anna said, "Coach Francine at Mommy CrossFit says that."

"Oh," Leen said, and kept it moving.

Dr. Burr got slow around floor five and Ally scooped her up in a firefighter's lift, no problem. By the fifteenth floor, the campers were sweaty and fatigued. This wasn't going great.

The countdown clock ticked in Wiki's head: **00:01:20:23**. "Come on, Blue Team!"

There were groans, but they pushed on. Floor seventeen.

Floor twenty. Floor twenty-two.

Wiki held up a hand, halting them. She heard footsteps. Someone or something was above them.

A voice called out, "If that's you, Pettygrew, you should know I've constructed an acid bomb that can melt any robot body you've taken over into sludge."

Leen?

"Hey, hey! It's Wiki, Blue Team, and Dr. Burr. You don't really have an acid bomb, do you?"

You never could tell with Leen.

"Wik!" was followed by a squeal as Leen descended the stairs in a series of half leaps. She rounded the corner to where Wiki and Blue Team perched by the big, stenciled *22* on the wall, then flung her arms around Wiki, who gratefully hugged her back.

"Where have you been?" Wiki asked. "But first, no acid bomb, right?"

"No acid bomb. I've been with Pettygrew. She's evil."

"We know. Don't know why though."

Leen craned her neck toward a gasping Petey, who was being held upright by the Mommy CrossFit Queen.

Leen said, "I have a good idea. Were you headed to the twenty-fourth floor?"

"Yep. You?"

Leen nodded and reversed direction. "We've got a lot to

211

cover, but not much time, huh?"

"One hour, seventeen minutes, and seven seconds," said Wiki.

The entire troop made it to the twenty-fourth floor, bursting through the door that put them on the far end of the false Fry Main Street the Thunkles had constructed. There were no PeteyTech employees fake-shopping this late. More importantly, there were no Pettygrew-possessed robots.

Archie's Hardware was still open, and its proprietor sat with his feet propped on the counter, while an old-school radio spouted sports stuff. Wiki, Leen, and the rest burst into the store, sending the door chimes into tinkling spasms.

"Mr. Archie!" Leen said. "There's trouble and we need gear."

"Finally!" The old man tossed his paper aside, sprang to his feet, and grinned. "Now this place feels like home!"

28

From Day One

Leen and Blue Team roamed the aisles with a couple of shopping carts, dumping in needed items as they found them. Not an easy task, since Mr. Archie had no discernible shelving system. There was no time for an extensive build, though. Which, in a way, made things simple.

Leen pointed out "We need things that can fight robots, things that can't be hacked," Leen pointed out.

They grabbed sledgehammers, rakes, shovels, a leaf blower that Britney insisted was more powerful than they thought, and other miscellaneous tools.

All gathered while the countdown continued in Wiki's head. **00:01:10:04**.

Leen wandered off with her own basket, isolating herself in the back corner of the store. Wiki left the Blue Team, all too aware that time was of the essence. Whatever. She was *going to* make time for her sister.

Leen sat amid a scattering of parts, oil, and compressed air tanks, working fast, with nimble fingers. Wiki was awed, as always, by what her sister could improvise in moments with whatever was at hand. Leen's usual joy was missing, though. While she worked, tears streamed down her cheeks.

"Hey," Wiki said. "What's up?"

"This will help you and your team stop whatever Pettygrew's up to."

"You say that like you're not coming with."

"They wouldn't want me there if they knew what I've done. You wouldn't either."

Wiki sat cross-legged outside the perimeter of parts Leen had surrounded herself with, like a makeshift fence. Leen wouldn't make eye contact.

Leen said, "Please don't ask."

"I wasn't going to *ask* anything. I want to tell you a story. It's about the day we were born."

"Are you going to tell Daddy's story? About me creepy laughing? Because that story doesn't make me feel good."

"No. This is a part you've never heard before. I'm going to tell you why I *wasn't* crying."

Leen looked nervous.

"Remember when Kelvin asked how far back I can remember? Well, I can remember way, way back to when

214

we were inside Mama's tummy. Let me tell you, it was pretty boring. I would've hated it if I were alone, but I wasn't. You were there, and we hugged all the way up until it was time to go. I went first because you were a big napper, and I didn't want to wake you. When I got outside, it was bright and loud and cold. I didn't like it much. A nurse was cleaning me up and said she didn't know why I hadn't cried yet. I wasn't super good at using my mouth and saying stuff, so I couldn't tell her the answer. You know what it was?"

Leen shook her head.

"I wasn't concerned with crying because I was afraid you weren't coming."

They locked eyes then. Their vision blurred through swelling tears.

Wiki said, "They're my team, but you're my sister. Doesn't matter if we're fighting. Doesn't matter if we're apart. I'm picking you first every time. Ever since day one. Okay?"

Through a sob, Leen said, "Okay."

Wiki stood, swiping away tears with her sleeve. "Finish up. I'll check in with the others. Then let's go do something epic."

"Say less, Wik."

The Blue Team, Anna, Mr. Archie, and Ally maintained an audience's posture while Dr. Burr and Petey engaged in a heated conversation.

"You're a government spy?" Petey said. Angry and hurt. Like he had the right.

"Not a spy. An *officer* from a bureau that investigates science crimes. Way more than what you and your company allowed me to be." Dr. Burr crossed her arms and stomped her foot. "How dare you act indignant, as if you're not the science criminal here!"

"I didn't know there were laws against giving my younger self advanced ideas."

"If you don't know dognapping is a crime but you kidnap a dog, you're still a dognapper."

Petey seemed to shrink to half his size. "Am I going to jail?"

"That's my preference."

Anna leapt forward. "Wait a minute. You're not a judge or a jury, Burr. We have the best lawyers around. We'll fight."

"Bring it!"

The argument devolved into yelling and accusations. Kelvin tipped his chin toward Ally, a signal.

Ally's lips morphed into the shape of a whistle, and her janitor's uniform shifted into the striped top and black pants of an NFL referee. The whistle's shrill note silenced all.

Ally stopped whistling and morphed into her previous form.

Petey scrutinized Ally. "Nanotech. Shape-shifting, adapts to any situation." He pointed at Kelvin. "You built this?"

"Sure did."

"How?"

Kelvin began to speak but seemed to think better of it given who was asking. "I think I'll keep that to myself."

Enough distractions. Wiki said, "We've got a little over an hour before the Interstellar-Z launches on Pettygrew's orders, and we're pretty sure she plans to pilot it through the big-time portal. Why she's doing it, we don't know, but it seems unlikely it'd still be on the ground if she could launch it sooner. Would you all agree?"

Britney said, "No matter what, the shuttle's gotta be fueled, inspected, and final calculations for the flight path have to be updated for the new launch time. You taught us that, Dr. Burr."

Dr. Burr nodded, clearly proud. She redirected her attention to Petey. "Do you have any clue what she wants? She's your assistant."

"I might." He wrung his hands. Nervous.

Everyone waited. None with less patience than Dr. Burr, whose stare could've melted steel.

He said, "Okay, okay. Pettygrew was one of my original good ideas."

Dr. Burr nearly exploded. "*I* reverse engineered the Roomba you put her in, and *I* handed over my artificial intelligence notes."

Petey held up his hands defensively. "I'm not trying to take credit for what you've done. I absolutely used your work to *improve* Pettygrew. She existed, in a simpler form, before you and I ever met, though."

Wiki said, "Simpler how?"

"Well, in the beginning, I built her into a toaster because I'm particular about the precise level of browning I get. You see, if it's a little too brown, then I have to scrape the bread, and I get these little gritty crumbs in my strawberry jam—"

Anna made a time-out T with her hands. "Hold on. Just so I'm clear. You created an advanced artificial intelligence to make your toast, then upgraded her to a vacuum."

"Yes."

Mr. Archie, who'd been quiet, let loose a dry chuckle. "Son, I've never been one for a lot of high technology, but even I get why your invention hates you. But please, go on . . ."

"She didn't even have a name originally," Petey admitted. "Only a designation code: PT-1000. Aside from making toast the way I liked, she also served as a sounding board for ideas I wished I'd thought of when I was young. I was close to building my first time machine in my mom's basement based on what I'd been through with the Legendary Alston Boys. I was concerned, however, that I'd only get to make one trip. So I wanted to get as many good ideas down as possible."

"You mean steal as many good ideas as possible," Dr. Burr corrected.

Petey did not try to defend himself. "I used PT-1000 to help narrow down the hundred best ideas. Not just based on the money I could make, but on the impact they could have on the world. The things that would let generations forever know that Petey Thunkle made a difference and—"

He stopped abruptly. Looked straight up, like he could see through the ceiling.

"Oh no." Petey jogged to the entrance of Archie's Hardware, then jogged back to the group, like he didn't know what to do with himself. "I know what Pettygrew's doing. We gotta get down to Mission Control fast. Faster than fast."

"I got that covered." Leen emerged from the back of the store lugging her newest gadget.

It looked like a harpoon gun. And a winch. There was a propane tank attached to it. Oh, Leen.

Petey evaluated the invention. "That's maybe a little faster than necessary. But okay."

Time Will Tell

They crossed the street to the City Theater. The real one, in real Fry, had an old-school box office where a clerk in a regal burgundy vest with golden braided tassels on the shoulder and a pillbox hat tore your ticket and showed you in. Beyond the doors, the air was deliciously buttery from decades of perfectly popped corn. There were two auditoriums, one always played a classic movie—sometimes so old it didn't even have color—while the other played the newest and best family films. Wiki and Leen usually found trips to the theater a comfort. Not tonight.

Petey voiced his fears on the move. "Pettygrew is angry with me big-time, so she'll likely go for big changes. The farther back in time she travels, the more drastic the changes to the present will be."

"That's chaos theory," Sierra said, "the butterfly effect. The idea that the fluttering of a butterfly's wings can change atmospheric conditions enough to cause a tornado in a different part of the world. I love chaos."

The other members of the Blue Team stared at her skeptically.

"I mean until now." Her cheeks blazed with embarrassment.

Petey said, "You are correct. I never went earlier than my high school years, though she encouraged me to. I felt it was too much of a risk to change things prior to what happened with me and the Alston Boys. I don't think Pettygrew has such concerns.

"When I was trying to narrow down the top hundred ideas I'd focus on, she suggested I build my Egg as it is. She provided the schematics and I never questioned her because she was mine. It was her suggestion we get into rockets and space travel. But now, I don't think space was ever her real goal."

Wiki and Leen got it at the same time. Spoke over each other. "She wants to—"

They stopped.

Wiki said, "You got it, Leen. Tell them."

Leen took a deep breath, slowed down to make sure she was understood. "Pettygrew's going to insert herself and the

Interstellar-Z in the past. The farther back, the more impact she'll have on our present."

They crossed the threshold into what should've been the theater lobby, but there was nothing. No *inside* to this building, only empty floor space and wooden support struts that kept the pretend building front standing upright, like the background in a play.

Several yards beyond the backdrop supports were windows, painted over in sky blue to aid the always sunny, always pleasant feel of the floor.

Kelvin, considering Leen's theory about Pettygrew's motives, said, "She couldn't go back so far, right? Go back before the internet and she's trapped in the shuttle. Before electricity, and she wouldn't be able to function beyond the life of the shuttle's battery reserves."

Britney held up a finger, though she looked deep in thought. "Not exactly true. Yes, prior to the internet and electricity, she'd have a hard time functioning as an AI assistant. It doesn't sound like she's trying to assist humans anymore. She wants to—"

"Fundamentally alter human history," Dr. Burr said, shuddering.

"I don't understand," said Anna.

Wiki and Leen dropped their heavy gear, and Wiki tipped her chin to Petey. "You understand. Explain it to your wife, sir."

Petey combed his fingers through his hair hard enough to tear strands loose. This was obviously difficult for him, being the engineer of humanity's potential undoing. "Ummmm. Yeah. See Pettygrew knows she doesn't have to function, at least for nothing more than a short time, and there'll be plenty of ways she can go into hibernation to conserve energy—for millennia if necessary. Even if she wears out all the available reserve power in the shuttle to near nothing, it won't take long to accomplish her goal."

Anna rubbed circles on her bulging belly, anxious. "Keep going. Act like me and our baby don't live inside your techy brain."

"Say Pettygrew and the Interstellar-Z are discovered by an early civilization, and she awakes long enough to explain fire or the wheel. Put aside the fact that early humans have stumbled upon a shuttle and all its accompanying tech, her providing them with those essential tools before they are ready would change how they develop. Say it was later than that, but she met humans who'd one day become what we know as ancient Greeks. What if she presented their own philosophies to them centuries before they would've developed them on their own? Maybe instead of Zeus sitting atop Mount Olympus, we get Greek sculptures of Pettygrew atop Mount Pettygrew."

Dr. Burr said, "She could introduce atomic science in the

fifteenth century. Or whisper the secrets of cellular technology to Alexander Graham Bell. Whatever she did, she'd be making herself the innovator that humans would laud forever, and there's no telling what unintended consequences that might have. Introduce the wrong bit of advanced science to the wrong person and the results could be catastrophic."

Petey scratched his chin. "I am now seeing why your Science Filcher's Bureau has beef with me."

Dr. Burr popped him in the back of the head.

Wiki said, "So. We're not going to let Pettygrew have her way, then. Are we?"

"Nope," Leen said. She was disoriented by pretend Fry, so she double-checked with Wiki. "This is facing Interstellar-Z Mission Control, right?"

"Yep," Wiki confirmed with her internal compass.

Leen said, "Awesome! Ally, break the window."

The machine lurched forward, anxious to comply. Dr. Burr threw her hands up. "Whoa, whoa, whoa."

Leen braced for an argument.

"Safety goggles." Dr. Burr dug into the canvas sack she'd taken from Archie's Hardware and distributed eyewear to everyone but Ally.

The machine's fist morphed into a hammerhead and punched at the painted glass. It was thick, reinforced, so it buckled outward instead of shattering and required several robo-powered swings. By the fifth strike, the entire floor-to-ceiling pane broke from the frame and drifted down before shattering on the pavement. Now there was a twenty-foot-tall rectangle of night in the midst of a spring sky mural, with hot, heavy wind howling in at them.

Petey inched to the opening, leaned out a bit, and craned his neck up. "The time portal's almost big enough for the shuttle."

"All righty!" Leen hoisted her harpoon winch gun onto her shoulder. It was bulky, so Wiki got shoulder to shoulder with her sister to help carry the weight. "Everyone stand back!"

The girls were given a wide berth as Leen stood at the edge of the drop and aimed at the Mission Control rooftop.

She flipped the Go switch and . . . nothing.

Leen frowned. Wiki glanced to the device, surprised.

Everyone else passed *is that it?* looks among each other.

Petey drew closer. "Maybe I should take a lo—"

Twin plumes of fire gushed from vents on either side of the blaster as one spike fired from the front on a forty-five-degree downward angle while an anchor fired upward from the back.

Everyone but the Epic Ellisons leapt backward several feet, startled. Petey landed on his butt with an *oof*, his face covered in soot.

The anchor spike punched through the ceiling and planted itself solidly somewhere on the twenty-fifth floor, while the front harpoon trailed loose rope that unspooled from a big spindle mounted atop Leen's device. A moment later, the projectile struck the Mission Control roof. The spindle tightened until the rope was a taut zip line, as straight as a geometry problem.

Britney had a shopping cart full of improvised zip-line trolleys made from pipe along with safety harnesses made from canvas straps.

Anna, who kept her distance from the howling hole in the building, expressed amazement. "You made all this in under an hour?"

Leen attached the trolleys to the line. "I know. Not my best work at all."

Anna rubbed her belly, wide-eyed.

Wiki stepped into a safety harness, cinching the straps tight around her hips, waist, and shoulders. "Not gonna lie to y'all . . . this part's really dangerous, so if you don't wanna come, we understand."

Dr. Burr said, "Should *you* be going?"

Leen looked appalled. "Dr. Burr, this is what we do."

Kelvin, Britney, and Sierra converged in a momentary huddle. They broke, and Kelvin said, "We're in."

Dr. Burr said, "Are you now?"

"Well," said Kelvin, "we trained for a lot of weeks to either pilot a shuttle or run mission control."

"A simulation."

"Yeah, but simulation or real, you need a team to complete

big tasks." He motioned to the rim of the portal widening over their heads. "What's bigger than that?"

Dr. Burr fidgeted, reluctant.

To speed her up, Wiki said, "We now have less than forty minutes until the Interstellar-Z launches. No one is coming to help us."

Leen said, "It's a little like being in space, right? You have to fix your own flat tire. Or whatever."

Dr. Burr nodded and claimed a safety harness. "I'm going first."

She grabbed a second safety harness and shoved it into Petey's chest. "You second. Then the children."

Petey, looking slightly green, didn't argue.

Strapped into her harness, with her trolley T-bar gripped tight, Dr. Burr stepped out of the twenty-fourth floor of PeteyTech Tower and sailed down the zip line, squealing. Petey followed. Then Wiki, then Leen, then the rest of the Blue Team, with Ally morphing her hand into a nano-trolley so she could follow.

When all landed safely, they waved up at Anna and Mr. Archie. Hopefully they'd all see each other again in a world they still recognized . . . if whatever Pettygrew planned didn't wipe them out of existence.

Time would tell.

00:00:38:02

30

The World According to Pettygrew

The Interstellar-Z loomed in the distance. Its corn-yellow sides looked sickly in the moonlight. Pettygrew's robots skittered along the scaffolding like ants in an ant farm, completing whatever work she'd deemed necessary before liftoff. While Wiki, Leen, and the rest couldn't see much of anything the automatons were doing from this distance, one big change was apparent.

The ship's previous designation—Interstellar-Z—had been painted over. Replaced with the word *Pettygrew-Z*.

The team freed themselves of their zip-line harnesses and wielded their makeshift Archie's Hardware weapons as they approached an access hatch on the Mission Control roof. Ally ripped the locking mechanism free and flipped the hatch open.

Dr. Burr said, "Ally goes first, then me and Petey. We'll do a little recon to determine what kind of opposition we're dealing with down there. Pettygrew might have a hundred robots guarding the launch controls."

Dr. Burr didn't say the obvious. If a hundred robots were guarding the launch controls, then there was no hope.

The children agreed to wait. Ally morphed her hands into a rough approximation of boxing gloves and dropped through the hatch. Dr. Burr and Petey followed.

Leen looked to the wide time portal over their heads. From beneath, only the pulsing energy of its blue rim was visible. No way to tell what was on the other side. "How far back do you think she's going to take the shuttle?"

Wiki shook her head. "I don't know. But what if it's the eighties?"

"Daddy's favorite decade," Leen groaned.

Together, in an excellent imitation of Daddy's voice, they said, laughing, *"Y'all don't know nothing about that good eighties music!"*

Their laughter tapered when Kelvin pointed toward the portal, alarmed. "What is *that*?"

It was way up, obscured by night, so it was difficult to see, though Leen detected some*thing*. She tugged her goggles on and tapped the gauntlet to increase magnification. "Uh-oh."

Wiki said, "Elaborate."

Leen shoved her goggles to her forehead. "Pair of pterodactyls."

"What?"

The flying dinosaurs cleared the rim of the portal and swooped down past the lower levels of PeteyTech Tower before catching a tailwind and drifting west. The Cosmos Campers tracked the beasts until they were no longer visible in the dark.

"So . . ." said Leen, "not the eighties."

"Kids," Dr. Burr called from below, "get down here."

The campers couldn't move fast enough.

It was quiet in the Mission Control building. Air hummed through the exposed vents. The general buzz of electricity powering the lights was *loud*. There were no guards that Wiki could see—perhaps Dr. Burr already had neutralized the opposition, making it an easy night for everyone?

If only.

"Follow me," Dr. Burr said. She moved toward the mission control command center. Pushing through the double doors, she stepped aside so the campers could see the absolute horror of it.

The computer terminals had been smashed. Unsalvageable. Unable to interrupt any launch plans. Though the monitors still worked.

Pettygrew wanted an audience.

The screens flickered on, presenting Pettygrew's face like an IMAX movie. "Well, here we are. I shall gloat now."

Leen glanced to the corners of the room. Security cameras on either side remained functional; the red ring of lights surrounding the lenses glowed. They were Pettygrew's eyes. The better to observe her victory.

"Do you think I'd leave any opportunity for you to alter my plans? Not only have I ensured you can't interfere with my launch, I've blocked all access to my navigation programs. My shuttle will fly, and it will fly true."

"To the Mesozoic Era?" Wiki said.

Leen added, "Being an assistant to dinosaurs seems way less fun than being Petey's assistant."

"We could have a healthy debate about that," Pettygrew said.

Petey said, "Hey!"

"You're all very smart humans. If you know *when* I'm going, then you know my grand design. The further back technology is introduced, the more drastic the ripples. I will be there when the dinosaurs go extinct. When the first humans emerge. I will be a constant throughout your history."

Kelvin said, "You and the shuttle will be a piece of old junk to whoever finds you first. What if they can't understand what you are?"

Pettygrew said, "Not understanding something has never

stopped your kind from creating stories. Legends. Belief systems. I will be threaded throughout the entirety of human history. Perhaps jump-starting the technology revolution by a couple of centuries. The name Pettygrew will be whispered with reverence."

Leen understood what was at stake, maybe better than anyone other than Petey. Because as much as she hated to admit it, they were alike. They had to create. It was like things that didn't yet exist called them to the intersection of Dream and Real. Sometimes the things that called weren't good.

"If anyone's left!" Leen said. "I know a little something about technology gone wrong! Who's to say you messing around doesn't get the whole world blown up?"

It was hard to tell what might become of their discoveries. Impossible to control what others used those discoveries to create next.

But if there was no next . . . if Pettygrew undid it all out of spite for Petey and for what she could never be—human— every discovery that ever pushed humanity one inch forward would be for nothing.

Pettygrew's narrow-eyed gaze fell on Petey when she said, "No big loss. Much less carpet to vacuum."

Petey said, "You're really not going to let that go, are you?"

The AI turned, as if checking something just out of the monitor's frame. "Wonderful. My prelaunch preparations are nearly complete. For the rest, I'll only need a fraction of my robot helpers. Since I know you'll continue to be a nuisance no matter how futile your efforts are"—she faced them fully again, with her widest smile yet—"I'll send you some company. Toodles."

The monitor blinked off, leaving them in momentary quiet. Until the floor started rumbling.

Dr. Burr grabbed the nearest chair. "Everyone, help me barricade the doors and windows."

The robots were coming.

31
Mission (Out of) Control

00:00:21:02

While the others grabbed every loose piece of furniture and equipment to barricade the doors, Wiki dug into Leen's bag and fished out some sticky loopers. She threw one toward each corner, where they stuck to the wall and cut Pettygrew's camera access. At least she wouldn't be able to see what they were up to.

What were they up to, though? Wiki said, "Leen! Ideas?"

Leen didn't have any.

Wiki grabbed her sister by the shoulders, stared into her eyes. "You're not still doubting yourself, are you? I thought we covered this already."

"It's not doubt. I just don't see a good solution." Leen shook free, swept a hand toward all the smashed terminals.

Petey said, "You're right. We can't stop the launch. Even if we could repair any of these terminals, we wouldn't be able to change any of the navigation data in time. Pettygrew said she locked us out, and I believe her. She's going to launch, and she will take the ship through that portal."

Wiki was officially stumped.

Leen, however, perked up. Her eyes bounced around the room, frantic. She ran to the nearest terminal, swept aside a smashed keyboard to give herself a clear work surface, then dumped the contents of her sneak bag on it. There wasn't much to work with. A tiny tool kit, some spare batteries, and the device she'd taken from Petey when he returned from his last time trip.

"Petey," she said, "Pettygrew altered the Egg to trap you in the past. But she must've repaired it if it's functioning properly for her trip."

"Sure. What are you getting at?"

"This device, when working properly, allows you to send information that the Egg receives without issue?"

"Yes."

"We can't stop Pettygrew from launching the shuttle and taking it through the portal, but what if we altered the portal?"

"Yes!" Petey joined Leen at the workstation, cracked open her tool kit, and handed her a screwdriver while rambling.

"Part of the problem with my design is I could never come back to the exact moment I left. It's why I left Anna a note, for if something went wrong. There was always a possibility I'd be gone longer than I intended."

Dr. Burr and the others returned, their best barricade work complete. Though the concern on their faces cast serious doubt on if the barriers would hold.

The doctor said, "What do we have?"

"A slight chance," said Petey, passing Leen some wire cutters.

Dr. Burr looked to Wiki, who shrugged, just as clueless.

"Anyone care to fill us in?" Kelvin added on behalf of the Blue Team.

Leen's brow was furrowed, but she broke her concentration to say, "If we can't stop Pettygrew from launching, we can sure change where, or when, she ends up. Now keep the robots off us. The timing's going to be tight."

That was all Wiki needed to hear. "Blue Team, looks like we're mission control after all, only this isn't a simulation."

Sierra cracked her knuckles and shadowboxed the air. "Wow, I love science."

00:00:12:02

32

Whac-A-Mole

Wiki examined the work everyone put in buttoning up the building, cross-checking everything against her memory of their Mission Control tour.

She said, "Three ways in and out. How strong are the barricades at each entry point?"

"Pretty strong," Kelvin said. "We found two-by-four planks in a closet from some previous renovations and braced the doors first, then set up the blockades around the braces."

Britney chimed in. "We've turned the doors into immovable objects."

Sierra said, "Unless the robots are the proverbial 'unstoppable force,' we should be good."

They were definitely not good.

A pair of robot arms burst through the brick wall beside

the doorframe, bypassing all barricade resistance. No one ever said unstoppable forces were incapable of detours.

More robot arms burst through the walls in explosions of force and dust, clouding the hallway in swirling red haze.

Wiki grabbed a sledgehammer. "Y'all ever play Whac-A-Mole?"

She took a heavy swing and knocked a pair of robot arms off at the elbows. The sparking nubs retracted, and another pair punched two more holes. The entire eastern wall of Mission Control became a grabby-grabby nightmare as robot arms sprouted like weeds, groping for anything that got close.

Dr. Burr picked up a crowbar. Britney wielded hedge clippers. Sierra tied small wrenches to her hands like makeshift brass knuckles, while Kelvin wielded an intimidating piece of pipe. Ally's hands morphed into medieval-looking axes.

"Blue Team!" Wiki shouted, a battle cry! "Charge!"

The most brutal game of Whac-A-Mole ever was on.

Battered, knocked, crushed, and severed robot arms piled at the Blue Team's feet with speed and ferocity. Tussling with Pettygrew's robots felt like fighting a mythical hydra—for every arm they defeated, two more took its place.

The increase in robot arms wasn't simple force multiplication. A pattern was forming in the wall, a specificity to the holes the enemy created.

Wiki yelled, "Everybody! Back up, now!"

The Blue Team listened, and just in time.

The robots perforated a portion of the Mission Control wall, creating the outline of a door. There were no longer enough bricks to keep the wall whole. Broken mortar cascaded inward, a mini avalanche.

A bigger avalanche followed: a robot avalanche.

"Whack the moles!" Wiki shouted. "Whack the moles!"

The bashing continued. The Blue Team held their own, doing everything they could to buy Leen and Petey more time. They almost succeeded.

A single robot broke through their defenses, Pettygrew's nosy scowl lighting its facial display. Ally chased it, swinging her axe hand at its legs. The strike severed its legs at the knees, but its top section still had momentum. The torso flew several feet toward Petey and Leen, grasping on to a nearby smashed console to stay upright. It was close enough to see what they were working on. Smart enough to know they weren't done.

It screamed, "Launch now!"

The countdown clock froze at **00:00:04:14**.

It flashed once . . . twice . . . then reset to **00:00:00:00**.

The building shook with the force of the Pettygrew-Z thrusters more than a mile away.

A vindictive Pettygrew cackled! "We. Have. Liftoff."

33

Final Destination

Pettygrew's face disappeared from the robot's display, and the mechanical body went limp.

All the robot bodies powered down, becoming unmoving metal piles littered throughout Mission Control.

Pettygrew's consciousness was fully committed to the shuttle now, and it climbed in the distance, a billowing pillar of smoke and flame thrusting it higher and higher into the sky.

Petey said, "We still have time. The shuttle will need to get approximately twenty-four miles above us before it makes its turn. Then, depending on if Pettygrew's relying on the boosters or gravity to reach the portal, we'll still have a few short minutes."

"Her goal is to make the shuttle a discoverable artifact for early humans," Leen said. "If she's going too fast, the force of impact would destroy any remnants of the ship. She'll use the reverse boosters to slow down before passing through the portal. I'm betting on it."

"How can you be sure?" Wiki asked.

"Dr. Burr, you told us what it takes to get a ship back to Earth safely. Pettygrew's been paying attention too. She knows who's got the brains around here."

Dr. Burr nodded, and Kelvin slipped his hands in hers.

Petey backed off so Leen could work but seemed to see Dr. Burr with new eyes. "I should've paid more attention too."

Leen worked as fast as she could to get Petey's handheld operational again. When the device powered on, the shuttle had reached the upper atmosphere and was slowing. The monitor drones broadcast an image that looked like a still photograph, a snapshot capturing a brief window of weightlessness before the shuttle upended, reversed direction, and plunged toward Earth.

"Leen," Wiki said.

"I know, I know." Leen chewed her bottom lip, her thinking-real-hard tic.

"What's on your mind, Leen?"

"A couple of things. One, *when* should I send the shuttle? Almost any time in the *far* past would give Pettygrew exactly what she wants, introducing the technology way before it should exist, making her a bigger deal in the world.

Anywhere in the near past could create a catastrophe of a different magnitude. Like, say I make it so the shuttle crashes on this land in the year before Petey started building his facility . . . then he probably builds it somewhere else, and maybe we're never around to stop Pettygrew. And if I just close the portal . . ."

She let that hang because she didn't need to explain it. If she closed the portal, the shuttle would hit PeteyTech Tower like a missile. Pretty bad day for everyone on the PeteyTech campus.

So what was the play here?

"Blue Team," Wiki called. "On me."

Kelvin, Sierra, and Britney huddled up and fell into nearly incoherent mumbling. Phrases like "shuttle length," "speed of descent," and "risk of paradoxes" leaked out. Otherwise, there wasn't much sense to be made of it.

"Children," Dr. Burr prodded. "Shuttle."

The ship was about eight miles over the portal and closing the gap fast.

Blue Team broke their huddle, and swarmed around Leen, each of them giving a portion of a new Hail Mary–esque plan.

Britney: "You gotta change the destination and location just a little—"

Kelvin: "But only at the last possible second—"

Sierra: "We'll know right away if it works, mostly because we won't all blow up."

Finally, Wiki said, "You got this, sis!"

Leen pulled up the time destination interface on Petey's device. The shuttle was now three miles over the portal, and the reverse boosters were slowing it down, forcing some on-the-spot calculations from everyone because a room full of geniuses loved calculating stuff.

Leen kept her eye on the camera feeds, seeing their window of opportunity shrinking by the second.

Dr. Burr—the fastest calculator—said, "Enter this!"

Leen listened to the doctor's commands and tapped them into the interface. Her thumb hovered over the Execute button.

The shuttle was within a mile of the portal.

Three-quarters of a mile.

Half.

"Now!" Wiki said.

Leen tapped the Execute command.

In the sky above, electricity crackled as the portal shifted . . . and the shuttle passed through, as smooth as a high diver passing through the surface of a pool.

Then more electricity crackled as a second portal opened a little over a half mile above the first.

The shuttle plummeted from the second portal directly into the first.

It happened again.

And again.

Each time getting faster and the rate of descent continued to increase once the boosters ran out of fuel, putting the shuttle into free fall until it hit terminal velocity, though it would not crash the way Pettygrew intended. Not so long as the portals held.

Because what the Blue Team had calculated and what Leen had executed sent the shuttle into the past . . . *ten seconds into the past.*

Because time was fluid and kept flowing, each entry into portal one would spit the shuttle out of portal two *ten seconds later*, ceating a loop that had the shuttle passing in and out of the portals too fast for Pettygrew to do a thing about it.

Leen imagined the AI throwing a tantrum as she fell. And fell. And fell.

Kelvin asked, "How long can those portals stay open?"

Petey said, "Given the way the clean energy works in the tower . . . indefinitely. At least until we figure out some other solution." He looked to Dr. Burr. "I'd like to help be part of that solution. If your organization would allow it."

Dr. Burr said, "Is that so? Because I have a solution that you're not going to like." She explained what she had in mind.

Petey huffed. "No. No way. Absolutely not!"

"That's your call. But say, for example, you don't want to go to prison for the rest of your life. You'll consider my proposal."

Petey hugged himself, tears in his eyes. "It's so . . . *harsh*."

"Oh boo-hoo, you baby. You caused this."

Petey looked to Wiki and Leen for help. "Girls, you don't think Dr. Burr's proposal is a viable solution?"

Wiki considered. "It's proactive. You wouldn't be waiting for something to go wrong with the portals, which would undoubtedly happen eventually."

Leen said, "It would still be like the launch we'd all been excited about, just in reverse."

Petey went bug-eyed! "A reverse launch?! That's how I'm supposed to look at it?"

Kelvin said, "I should reiterate that jail thing my mom mentioned."

His arms spread, face strained, Petey was set to object some more, but Anna shouted, "Petey! Petey, are you in there?"

She and her father stepped gingerly over random robot rubble on their way into Mission Control. Mr. Archie surveyed the damage, whistled. "Woooo. We missed a party!"

Anna shuffled to Petey and threw her arms around his shoulders. "Oh, bae-bae, you're all right. I was so worried."

"I know."

Anna observed the monitor. "Why is the Interstellar-Z stuck in an indefinite free fall between two sky holes?"

"It's a long story," Petey said. "Our investors aren't going to like it."

Anna's hands rested on her stomach. Her eyes brightened. "Petey, Petey . . . she's kicking."

Petey placed his hands on Anna's baby bump and gasped. "She sure is! We might have a little soccer player on our hands, huh?" Petey looked to Wiki and Leen, Kelvin, and Dr. Burr. "I want to make sure I'm around for all those soccer games."

Dr. Burr said, "Should I start making the arrangements? The sooner the better."

Petey nodded. "It'll be painful, but let's do it."

Dr. Burr said, "Now to find a working phone. I've got a heck of a lot to pass along to the bureau."

Dr. Burr left Mission Control. While the Thunkles reunited, Britney, Sierra, Kelvin, and Wiki formed a loose circle around Leen.

She said, "I'm sorry camp got messed up for y'all. You probably would've been named flight crew, though. You're all very good at what you do."

Britney scoffed. "This was way better than some basic simulation. Sorry, not sorry."

Sierra rotated her shoulder, wincing slightly. "Heck yeah it was. I only get this kind of action in the secret martial arts tournaments me and my family compete in."

They all lived in a moment of awkward silence until Kelvin cleared his throat. He said, "Is this what it's always like for the Epic Ellisons?"

"Yes," said Wiki.

"Pretty much," Leen confirmed.

"Welcome to our world," the Ellisons said together.

34

A New Arrival

The next morning, when parents arrived expecting a seat at the Interstellar-Z launch before gathering their camper's belongings and heading home, they received new directions. The road to the PeteyTech campus was blocked; cars were turned around by men who wore black suits in summer and looked like they all got their haircuts from the same impatient barber. They flashed weird badges with a holographic logo.

The parents—some grumbling their confusion, others anxious with concern—found relief when they turned onto the appropriate side road, parked in a special reserved area of packed sand with the ocean water lapping a couple of hundred yards east of them, and found their children congregated there. The kids were chatty, while more men in black suits fended off the droves of reporters shooting video and shouting questions from behind barriers.

Wiki and Leen were sitting on their trunk, in an animated conversation with the others, when Daddy parked and Mama stepped from the car in a teal sundress and floppy straw hat. "Girls?"

They rushed to their parents—whom they had missed more than they knew until that moment—with Leen hurling herself into a Mama hug, while Wiki grasped Daddy, then they ran around the car's back bumper to swap parents.

Daddy, in his completely dad-like cargo shorts and shirt patterned with orange tropical flowers, smelled strongly of cookie dough. He passed Leen a crab plushie and pointed in the general direction of the sky above PeteyTech. "What is that? And is it going to cost me money?"

The Interstellar-Z remained in free fall between the two time portals, each entry and exit making a rapid-fire *fwip-fwip-fwip* sound barely audible at this distance.

"A problem that we're about to solve," Dr. Burr said. She offered her hand to Mama. "Hi, I'm Antoinette. You have some lovely daughters, Mrs. Ellison."

Mama gushed. "Thank you! We think they're special as well. Would you mind telling us what the heck is going on here?"

Daddy came around to meet Dr. Burr while the girls rejoined the Blue Team.

Britney glanced at her phone. "My peeps are like three minutes away."

Kelvin said, "That'll be everyone. We'll get started soon, I think. You nervous?"

Wiki and Leen shook their heads.

Sierra's eyes were moist. "Even though it was a little bit of a scam and robots sort of tried to kill us, I'm sad that we'll be the last Cosmos Campers."

They collapsed on her in a giant group hug.

"Don't be too sad," Kelvin said. "My mom says as part of his stay-out-of-jail deal, Mr. Thunkle will be funding legit science camps all across the world."

Britney said, "That sounds cool—oh, oh, Mom! Dad!"

She waved her parents over, and everyone gathered for the show.

They were on a hilltop two miles away from what Petey calculated (with the help of the Cosmos Campers) to be safely outside the blast radius.

"Everyone!" Petey said, some hidden mic amplifying his voice through equally hidden speakers. "My lovely family . . ."

Anna and Mr. Archie waved.

". . . my loyal colleagues . . ."

Dr. Burr and the black-suited government goons remained stone-faced.

". . . the bright minds of tomorrow . . ."

The Cosmos Campers struck poses like they were shooting an album cover.

". . . and my friends in the press. I know you were all expecting a shuttle launch today, but things have changed. For the better. Welcome to the demolition of my flagship PeteyTech facility."

Reporters immediately shouted questions. Camera flashes went off like fireworks. Petey stopped talking until they calmed down.

"I will take your questions after," he promised, "but in the meantime, let's crash a ship."

Petey's mic cut out, and he joined everyone who knew how this was supposed to go.

He attempted to address Leen, but Mama interrupted him to say, "Petey Thunkle, when you have a moment, I want to talk to you about why I can't plug earbuds into my ThunklePhone anymore. It's very annoying."

Petey forced a smile.

Leen rescued him. "We have to do that later, Mama." She tugged Petey along. "You ready?"

"Actually," he said, "they're your portals. You should do the honors."

Leen looked to Wiki for reassurance, as always. Wiki said, "Do what you do, sis."

The rest of Blue Team gave thumbs-ups, and Leen, feeling pretty dang fine, took the portal controls from Petey. "Petty-grew wanted a crash people would notice. Let's grant her wish."

Everyone took one last look at the Interstellar-Z. A spaceship that never saw space. *Fwip-fwip-fwip*.

Leen tapped commands onto the screen and thumbed Execute.

The entry portal blinked out of existence immediately after the ship passed through. Then the exit portal closed as soon as the ship came out. With no more portals, the only place left for the ship to go was the ground.

The impact was legendary.

The tower—which was fully evacuated overnight, as was everything else within the estimated blast radius—was nearly vaporized. The shock wave bulged outward, taking down Mission Control and the Interstellar-Z launchpad in one direction, while obliterating the Cosmos Camp Training Facility and Space Museum in the other.

Even from a healthy distance, Leen felt the explosion's nudge, like a giant beast breathing warmly on them all.

Wiki, feeling more sympathy for Petey Thunkle than she knew she should, said, "I'm sorry it has to be this way. Your campus was beautiful."

Petey, perky, said, "Oh, don't worry about it. I've got like five other business campuses in three different countries. It's all good."

Wiki immediately regretted her empathy.

"Gather 'round," Petey said, tapping his watch, which

detached from his wrist and hovered in the air by his head. "Selfie time."

Leen's head cocked. "What is that?"

"Did you steal it from anyone?" Wiki asked.

Petey blushed. "No. This is one of my own designs. I've always been good with miniature aeronautics. This smart watch can hover and take pictures. Very convenient for—"

"Just shut up and pose," Dr. Burr said.

Everyone—Wiki and Leen, the Blue Team, Dr. Burr, the Thunkles, Mr. Archie, Ally, and the parents—crowded in for the pic. The backdrop, a dark and swirling mushroom cloud over the rubble that was PeteyTech Tower.

Everyone said, "Cosmos!"

The drone chirped, and the picture was automatically ThunkleDropped to all nearby ThunklePhones.

Wiki looked over Leen's shoulder admiring how awesome the photo was.

"Oh!" Anna Thunkle yelled. "Oh, oh, oh!"

"What's wrong?" said Petey.

"I think," she said, "that the baby's coming."

"Oh!" Petey yelled. "Oh, oh, oh! Clear a path!"

He rushed Anna to their nearby limo. The vehicle—one of the company's flying models—immediately went airborne and zipped toward the nearest hospital. Just like that, Petey Thunkle avoided the press conference he'd promised.

One reporter remarked, "Even I'm impressed by that juke move."

With nothing left to see, the crowd dispersed slowly. Wiki, though, got frowny. Kelvin, as skilled at reading tics as anyone, noticed and said, "What's on your mind?"

"You."

A blushing Kelvin focused on his shoes.

Wiki didn't notice she'd embarrassed him, too focused on her sudden worry. "Your mom worked near the Egg and all that weird temporal energy for just a few weeks before you were born. It helped make you super ridiculously smart. Gave you a memory like mine."

"Yes," he said, then his face went slack, getting it. "Oh."

Wiki said, "Anna's worked next to the Egg for how many months now?"

"Come on," said Leen, "no way the Egg had a similar effect on Baby Thunkle!" Leen looked to a concerned Dr. Burr. "Right?"

THREE WEEKS LATER

Epilogue

The night before the Logan County farmer's market meant chores.

Ellisons' CORNucopia was a popular stand—the *most* popular if you let Uncle Percy tell it (though since he tended to sleep in the truck while Wiki and Leen did all the work, it was unclear how he knew that). The girls had already prepared and stored their various corn-based products for easy transfer in the morning. So these chores were secret chores—Wiki helping Leen prepare the robots their secret loyal customers preordered.

They were in Leen's work shed, which always smelled like machine oil and gummy bears. Leen hunched over an updated model of her most popular drone, with forceps and a screwdriver, adjusting the specialized tool her newest customer requested. "Incorporating a potato peeler was way trickier than I thought it'd be."

"Mr. Hannamaker's going to love it," Wiki assured her. She loaded a few of the finished drones into the fake corn basket they used to smuggle the robots without Uncle Percy's knowledge. Demand was high since they'd missed a bunch of weeks while at Cosmos Camp, and Leen had been playing catch-up.

They were happy to do the work, relieved even. Because the Thunkles had kept their word and erased the debts hanging over Mama's and Daddy's heads (Dr. Burr made it part of the conditions to keep Petey out of jail). So despite having to fulfill backorders, it was nice to think Logan County could come to them for all its robot needs for many, many years to come.

Wiki checked the messages on her phone. "Miss Remica wants a drone that kneads dough for the bakery. Can you do that?"

"Tell her I need two weeks, but I'll throw in a ten-percent off coupon and some cornbread for her patience."

Wiki thumbed the message. "Done."

Her phone chimed again, as did Leen's. The Blue Team group text, or the "Bloup Text" as Leen liked to call it.

Wiki said, "Sierra sent us a ThunkleTube video about a guy whose whole thing is getting stung by the most painful stinging animals on earth."

"Why?"

"Because she's a little scary? I don't know."

Their phones chimed yet again. Not the pleasant tone of an incoming message, but the blaring alarm from the Adult Detector. They were about to have company.

Wiki sealed the fake corn basket. Leen draped a cloth over the potato peeler robot and waited for the knock.

"Girls," Mama said. "Come outside. Now, please."

They emerged into the hot, humid summer evening. The sun sank, casting a golden glow over the fields. Between the shed and the house, a vehicle idled. Not the kind you'd usually expect in Logan County.

Uncle Percy, on a break from all his trucking, appeared on the porch, excited. "Who ordered the party bus?"

It looked something like a small mobile home but painted a sleek black with silver trim. The bass thump of music could be felt in the ground, but not the kind the hip-hop kids from Fry High blasted when riding around town. The song was "Old MacDonald Had a Farm."

The bus doors parted on a verse about cows.

Inside, purple and red and blue lights flashed in sync with the tune. Dr. Burr, moving like an escapee, about hurled herself down the bus steps with her fingers plugged into her ears. "Girls!"

"Dr. Burr!" Wiki and Leen said together.

"Huh?"

Leen pointed at her own ears. Dr. Burr got it and unplugged her fingers. "Sorry. Three hours of 'Old MacDonald' can get to you."

"What are you doing here?" Wiki asked. "Why were you listening to 'Old MacDonald' for three hours?"

More people descended the bus steps, providing clues but no explanations.

Kelvin. Whom the girls flung themselves at, happy to see a Blue Team member face-to-face.

"Why didn't you tell us you were coming in the Bloup Text?" Leen asked.

"Because it's classified."

They thought he was joking.

Then Petey Thunkle exited the bus, carrying a satchel overflowing with diapers, baby bottles, rattles, and an old-school scientific calculator. His clothes were wrinkled and covered in milk stains. His eyes were bloodshot, like he hadn't slept since the day they crashed the Interstellar-Z.

Mama said, "We can tell who the new father in the group is. Fussy baby keeping you up?"

"Fussy isn't quite the right word." He sat on the ground with his back against the bus's front tire, like he might take a nap.

Anna Thunkle exited next, and she wasn't alone. Cradled in her arms, swaddled in a lavender blanket and sucking her thumb was the newest addition to the Thunkle family.

Mama got giddy and met Anna on the ground. "*Wook* at that *widdle* sack of sugar."

Anna looked . . . distraught.

"Oh, I see. The adult female is replacing consonants in key words to illicit infantile laughter. How very clever. Yes, yes, 'widdle sack of sugar' is quite humorous. I offer, without a hint of sarcasm or remorse, the laughter you seek. Ha. Ha. Ha."

The voice was squeaky and high-pitched. It didn't match the vocabulary used. So many oddities clashed in those few sentences, it was hard to process.

Mama backed up a step, pressing her hand to her mouth.

"Who's talking?" Leen asked.

"Evangeleen!" the mystery speaker said. "Such a pleasure to be in your company again."

It came from Anna's general direction, but her lips hadn't moved. Unless she'd become very good at ventriloquism, then . . . Nooooo. It wasn't possible. Was it?

"Is Victoria nearby?" said the impossible voice. "At this angle my vision is rather obstructed. Mother, could you turn me?"

Anna heavy sighed and shifted the infant, fulfilling the child's request.

"Uhhhhh." It was all Wiki could manage.

The baby, whose name they didn't even know yet, eyed

the twins with a little too much awareness. It was like meeting the gaze of a full-grown adult who wanted to share all their years of knowledge with you, for your benefit.

Enhancing and finalizing the strange, strange moment, the baby said, "I love a good reunion, but might we go inside and chat? Trouble is a-brewing, as they say."

Daddy was focused on his crab cakes when the group filed in. He grumbled, "Was hoping to have enough for leftovers. Guess not, though."

Mama told him now was not the time to be stingy. She gripped his hand and led him into the now-crowded living room. The Thunkle parents took the couch. Wiki and Leen sat across from them. Everyone else gathered around.

The exceptional child said, "Father, might I have the calculator, please?"

Petey, looking totally defeated by life, handed over the ridiculously old device. Wiki and Leen expected this exceptional child to work the keys. To . . . calculate something. She only gnawed on a corner of the device, strings of drool soaking the buttons.

Anna, matter-of-factly said, "She won't tolerate her pacifier at all. Loves to gum that calculator."

Wiki said, "Are we going to talk about, um, I'm sorry, what's your name?"

Baby Thunkle stopped her gnawing. "I haven't decided yet. I'm partial to Petunia because I saw a petunia and became obsessed, but my parents advise I may tire of such a permanent choice made in haste. I'm going to evaluate my enthusiasm for the name on Monday and go from there." She resumed her gnawing.

Leen said, "Your Egg did this, didn't it, Petey?"

"It did."

Dr. Burr said, "That's not why we're here, however. This is . . ."

She'd brought along a tablet with a kickstand case that propped it up for all to see. A screen tap brought up a video clip. In it . . .

A polished oak podium sat before huge windows overlooking New York City. A woman stepped into frame, thumping the mic twice. She had to be close to Mama and Daddy's age, but also, she couldn't be. Because despite being an adult, she was also Leen's former, backstabbing teammate.

In the clip, the grown-up who couldn't be a grown-up said, "I'm Harlow Whistleberry, the chief executive boss of bosses, and I'm introducing the world to this new powerhouse tech venture that's going to make all the other basic tech nobodies bow down! Haters, behold Whistleberry Artemis Ryder Innovations."

Two men—who were also not really men—joined her

onstage: Pierre, older but not taller, and Chest, who was bald but still muscular enough to stretch the limits of his gray suit.

They nodded at the reporters with slick grins.

The press in attendance exploded with questions. Harlow gripped the mic with malicious glee. "That's all for now. But just wait"—she stared directly into the camera— "we're going to change the world. Get ready for W-A-R."

Dr. Burr paused the video. If Wiki wasn't mistaken, a tiny spark of blue lightning crackled in Harlow's pupil.

"That's a problem," Dr. Burr said.

Leen wrung her hands, her smile too big and too fake. "Seems that way."

"Evangeleen, this isn't your fault. It's *his*." Dr. Burr cocked a thumb at Petey. "You may have let them into the Egg, but there should never have been an Egg to begin with. Besides, they'd infiltrated Cosmos Camp with the express purpose of stealing PeteyTech secrets. They would've gotten what they wanted one way or another."

Baby Thunkle took a gnaw break. "The bigger issue is the nature of the secrets they stole. I estimate upward of one hundred highly dangerous plans, along with their practical applications, were taken."

Kelvin said, "That's a bunch of ways to mess up the world."

Wiki and Leen still didn't know where their guests were going with this. Why come all the way here?

Dr. Burr pulled a small case from her bag and set it on the coffee table. It was hard plastic and blue, like the best team the Ellisons had ever been on. She popped the latches and raised the lid for all to see. Wiki's breath caught in her throat. Leen's eyes bulged.

Inside were two holographic badges. This close, they could read the engraved writing below the emblem: *Science Filcher's Bureau.*

Dr. Burr said, "To combat this level of Science Filching threat, the Sci-Fi Bureau needs all hands on deck. That means you two. If you think you can handle it . . ."

Wiki looked to Leen.

Leen eyed Wiki.

In that way that twins do, a silent agreement was met.

And rest assured, the conclusion they came to was epic.

Acknowledgments

A huge thank-you to all those who worked to make *Epic Ellisons: Cosmos Camp* happen.

Editor
Weslie Turner

**Publishing /
Editorial Directors**
Mary Wilcox
Monica Perez

**President/
Publishers**
Suzanne Murphy
Jean McGinley

Art & Design
Morgan Bissant
Alison Donalty
Corina Lupp

Managing Editorial
Mary Magrisso
Josh Weiss
Erika West

Production
Nicole Moulaison
Annabelle Sinoff

Publicity
Katie Boni
Taylan Salvati

**School & Library
Marketing**
Christina Carpino
Josie Dallam
Mimi Rankin
Patty Rosati

Marketing
Lisa DiSarro
Robby Imfeld
Nellie Kurtzman
Emily Mannon

Sales
Jessica Abel
Doris Allen
Nick Calderon
Megan Carr
Rio Cortez
Savannah Daniels
Cheryl Dickemper
Heather Doss
Kathleen Faber
Emily Logan
Jessica Malone
Kerry Moynagh
Caitlin Nalven
Hannah Neff
Fran Olson
Andrea Pappenheimer
Jennifer Sheridan
Tim Synek
Megan Traynor
Jennifer Wygand
Susan Yeager

Audio
Almeda Beynon
Caitlin Garing
Nate Hunter
Abigail Marks

Subsidiary Rights
Jessica Berger
Cameron Chase
Melissa Hager
Rachel Horowitz
Sheala Howley
Theresia Kowara
Jeanne McLellan
Cassidy Miller
Alpha Wong
Beth Ziemacki

Family & Friends
Clementine Williams
Adrienne Giles
Melanie Giles
Britney Williams
Jaiden Taylor
Joseph Green
Louise Green
Meg Medina
Ellen Oh
Olugbemisola
   Rhuday-Perkovich
Dhonielle Clayton
Tiffany D. Jackson
Jeff Zentner
Dapo Adeola
Derick Brooks
Jason Reynolds
Kwame Alexander
Raúl the Third
Kip Wilson
Kadir Nelson

Film & TV
Jennifer Justman
Mary Pender
Jason Richman

**Andrea Brown
Literary Agency**
Jamie Weiss Chilton

**Speaking and
Booking**
Carmen Oliver

Can't get enough of Wiki and Leen?

Don't miss the original adventures in Logan County!

Read on for a preview of

THE LAST LAST-DAY-OF-SUMMER!

1
BTSFOASTG

FIRST OF ALL, GRANDMA'S TEACUP-PIG calendar lied. It said the last day of summer was September 21. Everyone already knew September was a bad month with no good holiday in sight after Labor Day. Fourth of July was at least two months gone; Halloween was more than a month away.

But the real last day of summer was the last Monday in August. Cousins Otto and Sheed Alston had known this for a while, thanks to the big red circle around the last Tuesday in August. Inside that circle, equally red and in Grandma's handwriting, were the letters *BTSFOASTG!*

When they asked about it, Grandma said, "It's an acronym. It means 'back to school for Otto and Sheed, thank goodness!'"

The boys began thinking of it as an ACK!-ronym, because it meant back to alarm clocks, and homeroom, and home*work*. ACK!!

In Logan County, Virginia, summer ended when school started. Tomorrow.

And, thanks to an unfortunate headline in the latest printing of the county's newspaper, Otto was not going to take it lying down.

"Wake up!" Otto said. He finished tying his sneakers with jerky, irritated motions and stretched one leg across the gap between their beds, nudging Sheed's mattress with his toe; he'd allowed his cousin to snooze long enough, given the circumstances.

Sheed said, "Ughhh! Stop."

Otto had risen with the sun, eager and upbeat, like most mornings. As was his habit, he padded downstairs in socked feet, eased Grandma's front door open, and plucked the latest issue of the *Logan County Gazette* off the porch. There was usually some mention of him and his cousin in the folds of the daily paper, some new clipping to collect. The county folk loved reading about their local legends.

But what he saw on that morning's front page would never benefit from his admirable scrapbooking skills.

He'd stomped back upstairs, got dressed in tan cargo shorts and his favorite T-shirt. It was green with big white block letters that read STAND BACK, I'M GOING TO DEDUCE! There was work to do.

"Come on, Sheed. It's the last day."

The angry air from Sheed's nostrils puffed the sheet over his face into a tent. "I know. That's why I want to sleep."

"You only want to sleep because you haven't read this morning's newspaper."

"I don't read any morning's newspaper. What are you even talking about right now?" Sheed burrowed deeper under his covers, like a mole in dirt.

All around, on haphazardly aligned shelves the boys had fastened to the walls themselves, amidst the model cars and their made-up superhero drawings, were souvenirs from all the adventures they'd experienced throughout the season. A mason jar holding a shiny, pigeon-size husk from a Laughing Locust. A lock of banshee hair that sang them to sleep whenever the moon was full. And many more things unique to—or drawn to—the strange county in which they lived. Of all the trophies, it was the two Keys to the City awarded to them by the mayor of Fry that filled Otto with the most pride. Until today.

He smacked Sheed's shoulder with the rolled-up newspaper, then peeled back his blanket. "You don't really want to waste time sleeping on our last day of summer—our last chance to have one more adventure before you-know-what starts." Otto refused to say the S-word. "Do you?"

"Yes!" Sheed covered his head with a pillow.

Otto yanked the cord that zipped their blinds to the top of the window frame, flooding the room with bright sunshine. Sheed threw his pillow. Otto dodged it easily.

Sheed said, "Fine. I'm up. What's with you?"

Now that he had Sheed's attention, Otto unfolded the offensive newspaper for his cousin to see. Sheed read it. Then groaned. Then smacked his forehead. "I can't believe you woke me up for this."

Otto turned the paper so he could reread the worst news ever, unclear why Sheed wasn't more upset. The headline read: EPIC ELLISONS RECEIVE THIRD KEY TO THE CITY!

"They broke the tie," Otto said, his gaze flicking to their meager pair of keys; they somehow seemed duller in this morning's light.

The Epic Ellisons — a.k.a. twin sisters Wiki and Leen — were the county's *other* adventurers. Some might say they were rivals. Not Otto, though. In his mind, the Ellisons were clearly the inferior duo. Otto might have to talk to Mayor Ahmed about handing those keys out willy-nilly. But in the meantime . . .

"Come on." Otto grabbed his notepad and tiny always-there pencil. "The Legendary Alston Boys never sleep late!"

"That nickname's stupid," Sheed said, not meaning it. "*This* Legendary Alston Boy does sleep late whenever his annoying cousin lets him."

"Exactly." Otto slipped on his backpack, cinching the straps tight against his shoulders. "Like I said. Never."

Sheed rounded the corner into Grandma's kitchen and found Otto shoveling a final spoonful of cereal into his mouth. He still wasn't happy being dragged out of bed so early, but had somehow managed to get dressed despite feeling all yawny and stiff. He'd put on jeans that were spotted with permanent grass stains and ripped at the knees, red high-tops, a white T-shirt, and his favorite purple Fry Flamingos basketball jersey (given to him by Fry High School basketball star #00, Quinton Sparks, after Sheed and Otto got rid of the ghost haunting the Flamingos locker room last fall). He flopped into his usual seat while combing a plastic wide-toothed pick through his (admittedly small, but growing)